A Feast of

Peonies

A Feast of Peonies

by

Larry Redmond

Penknife Press   Chicago, Illinois

This is a work of fiction. The characters, dialogue and events described herein are the products of the author's imagination, and do not portray actual persons or events.

ISBN 978-1-59997-030-1

Manufactured in the United States of America

As for man,
His days are as grass:
As a flower of the field,
So he nourisheth.

The Holy Bible
Psalm 103:15

. . . All flesh is grass,
And all goodliness thereof
Is as the flower of the field

The Holy Bible
Isaiah 40:6

I

You feel your legs begin to twitch under the covers. You open your eyes. It's light outside, but very little of the light is getting past the room-darkening shades. Nothing around you looks right. Your balance is off, and your head swoons. You look at the clock. It's in the wrong place. 5 a.m. You take a deep breath and exhale slowly. Then you feel the hangover right behind your eyes. What did you drink last night? Oh shit! Tequila shooters. You try to remember if you smoked any shit. It's gone. The whole evening is gone.

You feel a stirring next to you. You turn slowly to see. Yup, there's somebody there all right, huddled under the covers like dirty laundry. You ponder whether to leave her there asleep, or wake her up. She clears her throat. Damn, she has a deep voice. You peek under the cover. The girl is creamy white like she never gets out. She's lying on her stomach. She sure has a skinny ass. And she's small. She has a body like a little boy. A mop of brown hair covers her face. She rolls onto her back. The bitch has a dick!

You resist the impulse to shout. You don't want to wake her ... him ... it up. You vow never to drink tequila again for as long as you live. Ok. You've got to think. Maybe there is a reasonable explanation. Maybe nothing happened.

He rolls over and slowly opens one eye, then both eyes, then smiles at you.

"Hey, baby," he says. His voice is still deep, but now it has a whisperyness to it. He wants to sound sultry. He has a Puerto Rican accent. "Did you sleep well." He smells like a man.

"Who are you, and what the fuck are you doing here?"

"I live here," he answers, his smile still radiant. You wonder if his too even front teeth are real.

"Ok, then what am *I* doing here?"

"Getting ready to play mama, I hope."

"I don't do the mama thing," you inform him.

"That's not what you said last night."

"What exactly did I say?"

"You said ok."

"To what did I say ok?"

"I said I would suck you if I could fuck you. You said ok."

"I did?"

"You did."

"Did you do it?"

"I did it."

"I don't remember."

"Ok, I'll do it again." He moves towards you.

"No," you say, clutching at the covers. "I mean I don't remember saying ok."

"Well, how else did you get here," he asks. "You don't think I knocked you out and dragged you kicking and screaming, do you?"

"I'm not a faggot."

"And your point?"

"I'm not going to play mama."

His smile fades as he ponders a moment. He sits up demurely, and adjusts the sheet over his folded legs. His long fingernails are lacquered bright red. The mop of brown hair is long on top and sculpted down to a fuzz around his ears and the nape of his neck. You try to remember if you've seen that look on magazine models recently. His full lips are still tinged with the red lipstick that had been on them last night. He has a small gold ring through his left nipple. Didn't that hurt? Both his nipples are surprisingly pointed and pink.

You ask, "what's your name?"

"Phyllis."

"How old are you?"

"Old enough that you don't have to worry." His eyes are a deep green.

"I want a number."

"23."

"Ok, Phyllis, I'm sorry. I didn't mean to mislead you, but I am not gay."

Phyllis ponders a moment longer. "Ok," he says, "then you fuck me so I can come."

Before you can say no, he flips around and onto his knees. He slides his knees apart on the silk sheet as he arches his back presenting his rectum like a little pink flower. The dark hair running from his scrotum to his tail bone approximates the shape of a pussy. Maybe this won't be so bad. Is this what Reggie saw?

"Wait a minute," he says. He reaches a small bottle of scented oil from the bookcase that serves as a headboard, and slathers oil on his rectum. He smells wonderful. He reassumes the position, and pokes his finger in and out of it a couple of times. "Ok," he says, "I'm ready."

He cups his dick and his balls against his stomach so you really can't see them. From that angle, if you imagine it right, he looks a lot like a woman. His rectum looks just like a woman's rectum, and your dick gets hard. You cozy up behind him and rub the tip on the flower. It feels like a woman's. He braces himself so you can push it in. You push the head past the rim and he purrs. Using slow movements back and forth, you work it all the way in. You close your eyes. He begins to rock his pelvis in and out, and you rub his sides from his armpits to his hips. He feels just like a woman, but different. Not as soft. You reach around to caress her breasts. They're small. The nipples are firm. You flip the little gold ring up and down a couple of times. You run one hand down her stomach to her pubic hair. Her dick is hard and pulsing. It has oil on it, too. You cup the head and rub it slowly. Her rectum contracts like a pussy. You let your fingers ripple back and forth over the rim of the head. She sits up resting her weight on her arms, and you stroke her like you would stroke yourself. She's small, scarcely five inches. She comes and fluid spurts into your hand. Pulling her body flush against yours, you come and fluid spurts into her ass. You nestle your face into the side of her neck. She rubs her face against yours. Before you can catch yourself, you kiss her on the cheek. She twists around, and you kiss her full in the mouth. She gives you her tongue eagerly.

She feels your dick slip out of her and, careful not the kick you, she turns around. Her toenails are lacquered the same shade of red. That color would look great on a car. Positioned by you right leg, she leans over and slides your dick into her mouth. You lean back and rest your weight on your arms. You spread your knees. She cups the base of your dick and scrotum in both hands, and works them up and down to the rhythm of her head moving up and down. You come again and she swallows.

You roll to one side and drift into sleep.

The sky around you is green as are the grass and the trees. You eat the grass and your stomach begins to ache. The ache gives over to an irresistible urge to take a shit. You squat behind a tree and push out a foot long piece of shit. You wipe yourself with a leaf from a nearby bush, and drop the leaf on the ground. From the spot where you dropped the leaf, the grass begins to turn brown. The trees begin to droop, and their leaves turn brown as well. The sun is setting, and the red rays from the sun turn the sky brown. You look down at yourself, and there are maggots crawling from your dick.

You wake to the smell of food. Curry maybe? You look around the bed and see your clothes on the floor where you must have dumped them last night. You feel the need to cover yourself. You reach for your pants and, pulling them on, you look around the rest of the tiny room. Your head is clear now, too clear.

The bed isn't a complete bed, but merely a mattress on the floor. The six-foot bookcase at the head is filled with college textbooks, novels, photography books and knickknacks, candles, incense burners, figurines of Shiva Dancing and Buddha. There is another figurine, twice as big as the others. It has a garland of skulls around its neck. There's a picture of a couple holding a little dark haired child. The woman is looking sternly into the camera, her mouth set, her eyes sharp like the eyes of a wolf, a wolf that knows everything. You have trouble looking at them. The man is mousy. His head is turned away, and he stares off at something or nothing on the ground outside the picture. The child— it isn't clear whether it is a boy or girl— is being held up by both of them, but it is staring up at the woman. It's probably Phyllis. He has his thumb in his mouth.

A well-worn chest of drawers occupies the opposite corner. A large round mirror hangs on the wall above the chest, and the window next to the chest looks out onto a back yard that serves as a large garden and a parking lot for four old cars. There are a couple of throw rugs on the floor. The door just at the foot of the bed is closed.

You slip into your sandals and stand up to pull on your t-shirt. You look at yourself in the mirror. You can't even look at your own eyes.

Compared to Phyllis, you are tall, six feet two to be exact. And you are heavy, a hundred and ninety pounds. You carry more of it around your middle than you would like, but you've been too weak to change your lifestyle enough or long enough to get rid of it. Your legs and arms are long and muscular, so you give the appearance of being in better shape than you are. In fact, except for your mid-section, you look like an athlete. You don't deserve this body. Your skin is as dark as black soil freshly turned. Your face used to be lean and long. But now it is oval-shaped from the fat, and your nose is short and bony like a fish head. Your lower lip looks bigger than your upper lip because you have a pretty severe over-bite, and your eyes are heavily pigmented. You've never been referred to as handsome, but you have been told that your face has character, whatever that means. You wear your hair in a thick bush. You force a wide smile that flaunts a gold-capped upper incisor. The left one. Maybe it's the stark contrast between your pearly white and gold-capped teeth and your uncompromisingly black face that people find so interesting. You don't deserve this face, either.

Phyllis opens the door and looks in. "Oh, you're up," he says, "Are you hungry?"

"No," you lie. "I've got to go." You avoid looking at him.

"I'm a good cook," he says, "and I've just warmed up some lamb stew and rice."

"I've got to go," you say again.

"Will I see you again?"

"Probably not."

"What's your name?"

"You didn't even know my name?"

"You didn't know mine until after we were in the bed naked."

Some people find you intimidating, especially when they hear your name, Ashanti Ra. You take a deep breath, and you can feel the power of your name filling your body. People think it's a taken name like Kareem Abdul Jabar or Mohammed Ali. And they think that you are dangerous. You don't deny being dangerous, but the name was given to you by your parents, both of whom died in a car accident in France in 1947. You were seven at the time. They were both poets who lived in Greenwich Village, New York, for years before it became fashionable. They were well-traveled as well. If your name is any indication, they spent at least some time in Africa. You breathe in again to feel the power.

As a rule, you offer you name with a mitigating tone of voice that puts people at ease as they ponder its origins. This time, though, you spit it out like a barb hoping it will sting and offend.

"Ashanti, 'Shanti Ra."

Phyllis ponders a moment, then says, "'Shanti and Phyllis. I like it."

"There ain't gon' be no 'Shanti and Phyllis," you tell him.

"Why not?"

"There just ain't, that's all."

"Are you ashamed of me?"

"No, why should I be ashamed of you?"

"Are you ashamed of yourself?"

You pause, about to answer, then shake you head no. You look away.

"It's tough being honest," Phyllis says, "especially with yourself."

Again you pause.

"Let's sit down and eat something and talk. Fifteen minutes is all. After that, if you want to leave and never come back to come with me again, fine."

You try to breath in the power, but it doesn't work this time. It's like your lungs won't fill all the way up. You don't want to answer yes, but you can't answer no. He'll think you're ashamed and afraid of the truth. You nod your head yes, and follow him to the kitchen.

He serves up soup bowls piled with rice and brimming with stew, brown with chunks of meat and vegetables. He gives you mismatched silverware and a piece of paper towel. The steam wafting up is warm on your face as you lean over to smell the food. It has a mix of pungent smelling herbs that you cannot identify. Curry? Thyme? Rosemary? The smells are comforting, relaxing, forgiving. You dip some of the juice into your spoon, and sip it. The flavors bloom in your mouth like flowers. "This is *nice*," you say.

"I told you I was a good cook."

You begin chewing rice and carrot and chunks of lamb, scarcely listening, but the sound of your teeth crushing food doesn't cover Phyllis' voice.

"I try to be honest with myself," he says. "So I have no illusions about who or what I am. I am a faggot." You cringe and he continues. "I will always be a faggot. I like myself as a faggot. But I don't always like the people that I let fuck me." He pauses. "We talked a long time last night before I brought you home. And I liked you. I thought you were honest, too. Was I wrong?"

Does fucking a faggot make you a faggot? No! Hell, no! "I try to be honest," you say around a mouthful of rice and gravy. "You got anything to drink?" You flip the question off with exaggerated nonchalance.

"What do you want?"

"Ice water would be fine."

"How about some iced fizzy water?"

"Great. So what did I say that you thought was so honest?"

"It's not what you said, rather what you didn't say."

"Ok," you answer. "What *didn't* I say?"

"You didn't say get the fuck away from me, faggot." He begins wolfing his food, scarcely chewing any of the pieces. It like his mouth doesn't want to be bothered with food now. It wants to keep spitting words at you.

"Why would I have said that?" The words sound wrong. They convey more than you mean. He could think that they mean that you fuck faggots all the time. You throw down a couple of gulps of water, and stuff more stew and rice into your mouth. You mouth spits too many words.

"You truly don't remember, do you?" he asks.

"I truly don't remember."

"Ok," he says, "it went down like this. "I got to the Latin Club about ten o'clock, and I was dressed to kill. I had on my black dress and my black shoes and my gold earrings."

"I remember," you say. "It was so short, it almost showed the crack of your ass."

"That was the idea. Anyway, I saw you at the bar drooling."

"You *did* look good." You quickly stuff more food in.

"You offered me a drink and I accepted."

"I remember now," you say, trying to chew more and talk less. "I offered you a shooter, but you wanted something long and sweet."

"I ordered a fuzzy navel, and we talked."

"About?"

"Lots of things at first. We talked about the band's playing. We talked about stuff we studied in school. At some point, you got your nerve up and whispered that you wanted a piece of me."

"Did I know you were . . . you know . . ."

"Gay? No, not yet. I leaned over and kissed you."

"In the mouth?"

"With my whole tongue, just like this morning."

You don't want it to, but you can feel your dick begin to pulse.

"You took that as a yes, and you said you wanted to fuck. I said I would suck you if I could fuck you. You said cool."

"But I thought you were a woman . . ."

He holds up his hand to stop you. "Then I said 'Did I tell you I was gay?' You said, 'so what?'"

"But I thought you were a lesbian."

"In the taxi to my place, you pushed your hand between my legs, and rubbed me. You knew what you were getting."

"I remember thinking you had an awful lot of skin on your pussy, but I never for one minute thought you didn't *have* a pussy."

"We came here and went to bed."

"And you sucked me?"

"I sucked your dick," he pauses, "just like this morning."

You belch, breath in the power, and say, "I'm sorry, babe. I may have said it, but I didn't mean it."

"That's ok, *babe*, this morning was worth it."

He stands up and clears the table, and you watch as he leans over to sweep a few crumbs in the garbage. He's wearing that black dress again. You catch yourself tilting your head to see under it. You strain to look away, but you can't. As if on queue, he looks around and catches you looking at his ass. Shit! Without changing positions, he turns away, finishes with the crumbs, and places your bowl and glass on the counter. Then with a flourish, he hikes the hem of the dress up around his waist and arches his back. He looks back at you staring at his rectum. He leans forward and gaps his legs. You stare at him, then his rectum, then back at him.

"It's tough being honest," he says.

Still looking you in the eye, he stands up and lets the hem drop. He walks slowly around to your side of the table. His erection pokes out the front of the dress. He doesn't bother to try to cover it up. He turns his back to you, pulls out a chair, and puts one foot on it. With a more exaggerated flourish, he hikes up the dress, leans forward and arches his back, then spreads his ass. He doesn't even look around. He knows what you are going to do. She throws her head back and moans like a real woman as you push deep into her pussy.

II

Usually, it was you, Jame, and Li'l Bo. Jame was the oldest at seven; Li'l Bo was the youngest, five. You were cousins. They were first cousins; they were your second cousins. But at Big Ma's house you were more like brothers. Jame had real brothers, three of them. Harold Junior, who was older than Jame, and John and Wallace, who were both younger. But you were special. You were the Three Musketeers; you were tall in the saddle; you were Hoppy, Gene and Roy.

Big Ma was their grandmother. She was your great aunt. Back then, you didn't know what a great aunt was, so she was just Big Ma, the woman who was older than your own mothers and who told your mothers what to do. You threatened Big Ma once, back when you thought she was just another grownup. Big Ma had chastised you unjustly-- at least in your mind-- and you threatened to tell your mama. "*Ah'm* the mama around here," she told you. "Ah'm the *big* mama." You told your mama anyway, just like you had threatened. Mama laughed at you, and from then on, you knew who the real boss was.

You were also more afraid of her than your own mothers. Your mothers would coddle you, but Big Ma spanked, and you all knew it. You knew because she told you. "Don't play with me," she would say, "because I spank." You know now that it was a propaganda ploy, but it worked. You stayed on your Ps and Qs in that woman's house.

Big Ma was tall and skinny with big feet and big hands. They were strong hands from working in the cotton fields down south. She was flat chested and she had no hips to speak of. She had a long face with eyes that drooped at the corners. Her hair was mostly grey, but she sometimes wore something in it that made it look blue. For some reason, she thought that blue stuff looked good. Whenever she got the blue stuff put in, she would walk around with her head held just a little bit higher, like she thought she was a queen or something.

The genealogy went like this. Big Ma, a.k.a. Verlene Royce, had a brother named Albert Buchanan who was your grandfather. She had two daughters, Louise, who was Jame's mother, and Martha, who was Bo's mother. Her sons were Wallace, William, Albert and the baby twins, Collis and Reggie. Only the twins still lived at home.

The twins were 16. They were dark and strong and hansom. Collis was the good twin, the artist, the innocent one, the one who smiled and played with the young boys from time to time, and told you jokes. He drew pictures for you whenever you asked. He drew a picture once of a rose, and gave it to Martha. She has it to this day.

Reggie was the bad twin. He sulked and he rarely, if ever, played with you. He couldn't draw, and he resented that Collis could. You used to ask Reggie to draw pictures for you, but they were never the same. You never understood that Collis and Reggie were different even though they looked just alike. In time, Collis began to stifle his artistic talent because he knew it was a source of anxiety for Reggie. Reggie tried once to teach you how to play cards, but you were too young.

It was Collis who discovered the body in the basement.

During this particular summer, you were at Big Ma's house often. She lived on the second floor of a building on 35th Street between Calumet and Giles. Around the corner from her house was a vacant lot. This lot, covered with wine bottles and rusted out cans, broken building bricks and old tires, and overgrown with weeds and tall grasses, was the hunting ground. This lot was the jungle you stalked in, the war zone you fought in, the range where you wrangled and rustled cattle.

Back then, fruit was delivered in crates, cheap wooden crates nailed together with wire hinges on the lid. The grocery store near the lot discarded empty fruit crates out back two or three times a week. These crates fueled your creative powers in countless ways all that summer. Assembled, you used them as vehicles, houses, building blocks for forts, bombs. Disassembled, they supplied the raw materials-- the slats, the nails, the wire, the corners-- for countless childhood projects like crutches, swords or, in this case, your hunting rifles.

The rifles consisted of nothing more than a short slat nailed down to a long slat in such a way that the short slat swivelled like a trigger. You used bricks that were carefully "mined" from the lot to pound the nails into place. The bricks had to be clean, smooth, and devoid of the white, mold-like growth that was your clue that the brick would crumble if it were used as a hammer. The final piece was a cross-section cut from a car inner tube like a giant rubber band. You found inner tubes in the same lot, and used broken pieces of glass to cut them into strips. These circles of thin, pliant rubber were the bullets you used. The pieces of inner tube hooked around the front of the gun, then stretched back over the hammer which was really just the top piece of the wood that was also the trigger. The principal was exactly the same as shooting rubber bands with your fingers. When the trigger was pulled back, the hammer went forward releasing the strip of inner tube from the front of the gun. A good rifle could shoot a piece of rubber fifteen or twenty feet.

Once all of the building and testing and range testing were done, you started the hunt. This is the part where you crawled through the lot on your stomachs like soldiers careful not to disturb too much of the grass. The key was to wait for the prey to alight, then shoot it. You hunted butterflies and grasshoppers. The flight of the rubber bands was so unpredictable that you rarely, actually hit the mark. And if you did hit it, there would be so little force that the game would simply crawl from under the debris and fly or hop away.

More often than not, you would catch butterflies by stalking them slowly, sneaking up behind them, and pinching their wings between your fingers. Butterfly wings are fragile. Pinching them always left a white residue on your fingers, and usually crippled the butterflies. Sometimes, you would give a wounded butterfly to the ants crowding a crack in the sidewalk. At other times, you felt virtuous and humane in letting the critters go after having walked around with them for an hour or so, after holes had been eaten into their wings by the sweat between your fingertips.

Grasshoppers were different. You used the same technique, and pinched their back legs. But they were stronger than butterflies. Sometimes, they could snatch themselves from your grasp. When they couldn't, though, they would 'spit tobacco' on your fingers. You showed the 'spit tobacco' phenomenon to your mother, and she gagged. You did, too, when she told you the bug was having a bowel movement from fear. You didn't hunt many grasshoppers after that.

Being the oldest, Jame was the biggest. He was thin and brown with wide eyes, a wide smile and gaps between his teeth. Back then, you always wanted to be older than you were. You had been given a double promotion in school, and, consequently, you were always the youngest and smallest person in class. *Ergo*, you were always being picked on and teased. In you mind, being one year older would have made such a difference. Being one year older, you would have been less shy, more popular with the other kids, better able to fight back. Jame, by contrast, *was* one year older. He already was where you desperately longed to be. It always amazed you to see him cry, because he always seemed to have arrived at that magical point in the future when life was without problems. Yet, he cried a lot. He needed to cry as often as you did.

Maybe more. In fact, his left thumb was flat, shriveled, faded and always wet because it was always in his mouth because he was always crying.

Jame told fantastic stories with terrific sound effects. His primary character was Harry Hachmann, World War II Messerschmitt ace for the Third Reich. Harry came into being one rainy afternoon when you were playing with a couple of plastic model airplanes you had built. Jame had built a purple Messerschmitt; you had built a blue P-38 Lightning.

Naturally, the fiercest airwar in the history of aviation broke out in Big Ma's living room that very afternoon. The Messerschmitt won because Jame's sound effects were so much better than yours, the roar of the engine was so much louder and heavier, the bullets struck with so much more authority. Since it just wasn't American for the Messerschmitt to win most of the time, you changed planes. Now he was the Lightning, and he won *all* of the time. Finally, you decided that he should fly both airplanes, one in each hand. The result was magic. The planes dove and climbed nose to tail, wing to wing, sputtering, stalling, rolling first left, then right. Machine gun fire strafed the walls and ceiling and the big, black cast iron stove in the middle of the floor with such thunder and clarity, Li'l Bo and you ducked to avoid being hit. Jame twirled his arms like a windmill by leaning his torso at the angle, then spinning his whole body. The effect was stunning. In the end, the good guy won, but Harry Hachmann always parachuted to safety.

Your most vivid memory of Li'l Bo is from a couple of years earlier. He, his parents, your parents and you lived in a basement apartment on South Michigan Avenue. Li'l Bo was always wet and smelly and in need of having his nose wiped. You were always surprised when no one ever turned him down. No one ever helped you blow your nose anymore, but they always helped him. You resented that a lot.

You remember this period as much for a dream you had one afternoon when you were sick as for anything else. You had been sick with a high fever for what seemed like days. You were poor. Your parents had no money for a doctor. The reason they shared an apartment with Li'l Bo's parents is because you were all poor. In this dream, you wanted to leave your body-- for good. You opened your eyes from the dream, and saw your parents staring helplessly down at you. You knew what they feared, but you did not care. In fact, it seems the person who was you in the dream had left the room, and was headed for the 'other side.' The gatekeeper was an old, black man wearing a white beard and puffy, white hair, and dressed in white clothes. He nodded his approval for you to go. Then suddenly, he changed his mind. He summoned you back.

"But I thought I would never have to go back again," you whined in the dream.

He whispered something to you in your ear. The you lying sick in the bed couldn't hear what was being said, but you felt as if you were being tricked. But then the dream you expressed an understanding of the situation, and reluctantly agreed to come back to this side. "You've got a lot of work to do," the old man said. A day or two later, you were up and sipping soup.

Li'l Bo was really Bo the Third. His father, Big Bo, was Bo, Junior. You never met Bo, Senior, and you were glad that you hadn't. The reason is that you, too, were a junior. In your mind-- and Jame and Li'l Bo concurred-- 'the Third' was to 'Junior' as 'Junior' was to 'Senior.' 'Junior' was a lot bigger than 'the Third' because Big Bo was a lot bigger than Li'l Bo. 'Senior' was a lot bigger than 'Junior' because your father was a lot bigger than you. Therefore Bo, Senior, must have been as big as King Kong. The day you made *that* connection, the Messerschmitt and the Lightning fought on the same side to shoot King Kong standing wide-legged on Big Ma's couch. Good thing, too! Mouth bombs were no match for a belt.

Near the end of that summer, one morning over breakfast, Collis mentioned that he had seen someone tugging a trunk into the basement the night before. He was talking to Reggie and Harold Junior. One of them suggested that they go down and take a look. Collis wanted to call the police.

"Shoot," Reggie said, "Ah'm goin' down and look."

They didn't want him to go alone, so Collis and Harold Junior agreed to go, too.

The back yard was paved with concrete. The steps to the basement led under the wooden porches. Once at the basement door, Reggie began losing his nerve. He and Collis debated the wisdom of this venture while Harold Junior tried to shoo the Three Musketeers away. Naturally, you wouldn't be shooed. You were, after all, the Three Musketeers. Finally, Collis agreed to lead the way.

Reggie gave Collis the flashlight, and he nervously pushed the door open. They tiptoed in, and you tiptoed in behind them, close enough to touch one of them if one of you got scared.

The basement was cool and musty and felt good after being in the sun. The floor was cluttered with junk, wheelbarrows, bicycles, bed springs, hoses, pipes and rags. A heavy grime covered everything.

Collis spotted the trunk resting by the back wall. It was the only clean object in the room. His hand shook, and the beam went dim. He shook the light deliberately to get it bright again. He told Reggie to open the trunk.

"Ah'm not gon' open it," Reggie said.

"Here then, hold the light."

Reggie held the light while Collis approached the trunk. He paused a few seconds to steel himself. He pulled at the latch. It was stuck. Finally, it gave, and he pried the lid open a crack.

"Peek in," he told Reggie.

"Just throw it open," Reggie said.

He did.

In the dim light and between the bodies of the big guys in front of you, you only caught a glimpse of the contents. It was red, and you think there were some pieces. You tried to get a better look, but the beam jerked wildly before it went out, leaving you in pitch darkness, and the guys in front were nearly trampling you to get to the door.

Jame, Li'l Bo and you ran out into the yard. You thought Collis, Reggie and Harold Junior were behind you. By the time you looked around, they were half way up to the second floor going two and three steps at a time. You heard loud shouts from the kitchen, and Big Ma ordered you to come up, too.

Within minutes, the yard was crowded with police and on-lookers. From the porch, you saw them haul the trunk out to a waiting truck. The police came upstairs. It was the only time you had ever seen white people in Big Ma's house. They questioned Reggie and Harold Junior. They questioned Collis.

"Did you see who put the trunk down there?"

Collis paused. "Yeah, I saw him. He looked right at me."

You were with him that night, just the two of you. You were on the back porch breathing in the warm summer air. You felt special having him to yourself. And he made you feel special the way he rubbed the top of your head with his hand. He pointed out the brightest star in the sky and told you it wasn't a star. It was a planet. You wondered how he knew. You heard a scrapping sound. Someone was dragging something heavy down the alley is short spurts. Collis heard it, too. You both looked towards the alley, but the noise was behind the building. He pointed to the North Star and the Big Dipper and the Little Dipper, and you strained to count the stars in each. By the time you finished counting, the scrapping sound was in the yard below you. Collis stood up to see who it was. The pause in Collis' attention irritated you. You stood up too and looked between the slats of the back porch railing to see the charcoal grey figure of a man slowly dragging a trunk on the ground behind him. Judging from the way the man strained with each lunge, the trunk was heavy. His back was to you and Collis. He was pulling the trunk towards your building. You wondered what the man looked like, and just then, Collis cleared his throat. The man was caught completely by surprise. He spun around and planted his behind on the trunk and if to keep the lid from popping open. He looked wild-eyed from one porch to the next until finally he saw the two of you. He opened his mouth slowly, but he said nothing. He glanced again wildly from porch to porch and all around the yard. Then he looked back at Collis. This time the wildness in his eyes was gone. Now his eyes were cold like the eyes of a snake. The look in his eyes scared you and you hugged Collis' leg for comfort. The man narrowed his eyelids, and the muscles at the base of his jaw began to flex. Collis flinched. He was scared, too. The man jerked his gaze at you, and moved his head from side to side to get a clearer look, but the railing slats prevented him from getting a clear view. The man looked at Collis again as if to make sure he had the details right, then he wheeled around and pulled the trunk with renewed energy. The trunk thumped down the concrete steps that led to the basement. You had wanted to count some more stars, but Collis whisked the two of you back inside.

The police took Collis down to the station to look at some pictures. Then it was quiet, quiet as if things were normal, as if nothing had happened, as if no body had been found.

But they were not normal. Things were changed; Collis was changed. He didn't play with you as much any more. He didn't laugh and joke as much. All of a sudden, life was serious.

You don't remember hunting much after that day. Maybe life had become too serious to hunt butterflies. Or maybe Big Ma had decided the neighborhood had become too dangerous to spend much time outside anymore. Collis saw the man again more than once after that day, and he was afraid because he believed the man was stalking him. He stayed in the house a lot depressed. He notified the police each time, but they always came too late.

You saw the man just once after that night. There was a tavern down the street from Big Ma's house that was notorious for its loud music and the fights that used to spill out onto the street. Sometimes you could see the fights from Big Ma's front room window. People were always arguing in front of the place as well. Sometimes the arguments turned into fights. Or maybe they were just loud and determined conversations that used a lot of foul words like the one you remembered between a large, dark-skinned woman and a small light-skinned man. Watching from the window, you could see the woman towering over the man with her hands on her hips and her head moving from side to side. You opened the window a crack to hear.

". . . and motherfucker, I will kick your puny little ass." With that pronouncement, she hit him, and he staggered back a couple of paces. She reached to hit him again, and he pulled a straight razor from his pocket. He flipped it open. Now everything was different. The crude expression of contempt and loathing on her face quickly shifted to one of chagrin and embarrassment and fear. She looked around wide-eyed at the people who had gathered to watch her berate her man. She wanted to run, but after all that big talk, she couldn't. He slashed at her and she threw up her arm to block it and got cut on the forearm. A thin stream of blood appeared. He slashed her again, this time on the other arm. Another stream of blood. Now all of her pride was gone. She sank to her knees to plead with him not to kill her. He slashed her again on the first arm, then again. A piece of something pink fell away. He slashed her across the left side of her face. She collapsed on the sidewalk, resigned to her fate. Blood was everywhere. He looked down at her, then folded the razor and put it back into his pocket. The onlookers moved out of his path as he walked away.

Two weeks later, Big Ma and you were walking past that tavern on your way to the 'L.' The woman was out front again only a few feet from where she had been lying. She had white bandages from her wrists to her elbows on both arms and a bandage on her face. She was laughing loudly and drinking with the man you and Collis had seen from the porch. He was laughing and drinking, too, until he realized that you were staring at him as Big Ma dragged you along behind her. He must have recognized your eyes, because he stopped talking mid-sentence. He stopped laughing, too, and returned your stare. You turned to get Big Ma's attention. When you turned back around, he was gone.

Collis and Reggie began to exchange clothes whenever they went out. They were, after all, twins. Maybe the man would be fooled. Then one day, the man *was* fooled. He saw Reggie dressed like Collis, and chased him for half a mile before Reggie got away. Reggie ran into the house terrified. He told Big Ma and Collis what had happened, and Collis sighed as he made up his mind to stop living in fear. He made a supreme effort to be his old self again. No more hiding inside; no more exchanging clothes.

That winter, Collis was killed. He had gone to ice skate with some friends on a patch of ice near the butterfly lot. He skated around for awhile, playing tag with his friends on the ice, flying back and forth as if it were summertime. He stopped to rest, poised on a log at the edge of the ice. Just then, someone shot him. His friends thought he was clowning, thought he had fallen off the log for sport. When they couldn't get him up, they called the police who came to take away the body. They questioned his friends, but nobody saw anything. Or if they did, they certainly were not talking.

Some say he was killed by the man he had seen tugging the trunk to the basement. Others say he was just at the wrong place at the wrong time. As far as you knew, neither crime was ever solved.

III

"Mmmm," she says, "what's the meaning of this?" Her voice is throaty and low. You remember how low Phyllis' voice was.

"The meaning of what?" you ask back sliding your hand from one breast to the other. Rubbing her cleanses you, makes you feel right again.

"The meaning of all this rubbing?"

"This is the precursor to an earthquake."

"An earthquake?"

"Yeah, you know," you say, "one of those things that rattles buns and makes the bed bounce."

"The folks in California could sure use a person like you."

"I wrote 'em a letter," you say. You roll onto her body, and she takes your tongue deep into her mouth. Now this is the way it is supposed to be.

Jean Dobson and you have been seeing each other for some years. You've always liked that expression, "seeing each other." It always elicits images of rubbing eyeballs or something, when as a point of fact, eyeballs are probably the only things you had not rubbed. Well, so far, at least.

You met her in an Old Town folk guitar class one Friday. You had been tired of moping around the house wishing you could meet someone, tired of watching reruns on television. What is it that finally sparks action in a person? The pitying glance of a stranger? The rapture on the countenance of the successful? The disappointment in one's own eyes? Whatever it was, it worked. You had always wanted to play blues guitar, so you signed up for a class. She wanted to play Joan Baez, and eventually she went on to become pretty good. You went on to dabble in jazz piano.

That night, she wore a pair of pink jeans and a blue denim jacket. She had her guitar strapped to one shoulder in an army green canvas carrying case. That was ten years ago, and she looked like she had just stepped out of the heyday of the hippie era.

She saved your life that night. She slung her guitar off her shoulder and propped it against the wall like a soldier might prop a rifle. She plopped her jacket on the floor beside an empty chair, sat cross-legged on the jacket and poured herself into the fingering of a G chord. She used to refer to the way her fingers looked while fingering her instrument as chicken claws. The image was a good one because her hands were bony and white with tendons protruding at the back. The skin looked cold and pale like that of a newborn. She never liked her hands, but they always struck you as being agile and utilitarian. It was her hands that night that drew you to her. To you, a person with hands like that had substance, real flesh and blood. These were the hands of someone who liked to fuck and groaned when they did it, not the manicured, polished hands of someone who did it out of duty and signed through it all. You could speak your mind to a person like this and not be afraid of bruising her sensibilities. These were the hands of a real woman.

Your conversation with her pumped new essence into your lungs and blood and brain. You could feel the cells waking up to new possibilities. Life didn't have to be lived longing for elusive and ethereal love. Chords led to coffee after class which led to a set at Blues Chicago. Was it luck or predestination? Did it matter? She was there. Her breath on your face dried the water in your lungs. You could breathe and breathe and breathe.

She was five feet, six inches tall, which you'd been told was average for a woman. But she was a full head shorter than you, so you always thought of her as short, especially for a lifesaver. Her body had and still has lots of soft curves. It isn't angular like some of the athletic types who seem to glory in having bodies like men, nor bulging like others you've seen who glory in having bodies like bags stuffed with cotton. Voluptuous is the word. And she carries herself with an air of carefree abandon that enhances the hippie image. No girdles and no bras! Those sure were the days!

Unlike her body, her face is angular. She has a square jaw and a pointed chin, and she wears her flaming orange hair pulled back away from her face revealing a hairline that veritably zig-zags across her forehead. Her eyes are close-set and green, flecked with tan like cat-eye marbles. Was it her keen eyesight that enabled her to see you drowning out there on the horizon? Her lips are thin ridges like chisel cuts in soapstone. The overall effect is softened by the downy hair that covers her cheeks, the wispy, fine blondish hairs that curl in front of her ears and over her widow's peak, and the mass of freckles that color her nose and cheeks, especially in the summer. She saved you then, and riding her has always been a renewal for you. Her soft body under you has been a balm for your mind, your body, your spirit for years.

"You are really hungry this morning," she says. "Are you trying to prove something? I mean, we both already know that you are a man. In fact, you are *the* man. So what's up?"

You roll off of her. This time, there is only so much the balm can do. You look at her, at the pink nipples on the milky breasts, at the skin on her neck beginning to look like chick skin.

"What's the matter?" she asks.

"Nothing," you say.

"You're not still upset about the other night, are you? Because I'm not. At least not much. I mean . . .."

"I'm not still upset."

"So where did you go?"

"I went to the Latin Club and got drunk."

"And you were gone all day yesterday."

"Getting over the hangover."

"Did you meet someone new?" She tries to keep the anxiety out of her voice.

"No." You try to keep the anxiety out of yours.

"So what's the problem?"

"Nothing," you snap, and roll out of bed under the guise of going to the bathroom. The ache is too deep. The last thing she needs to know is that you spent the night with some man, even if you didn't get fucked.

The problem is that she lies. She lies to you; she lies to herself. She says she isn't upset about the other night, but that's a lie. Sure, you lie, everybody lies, but she lies more than everybody you know. But maybe she isn't lying. Maybe she's just trying to be positive. Maybe the root of her lying isn't dishonesty, but an attempt to alter the facts, alter the truth. If you tell a story long enough, it becomes the truth. Maybe she was merely telling a story. Maybe your distrust of her isn't justified. Maybe it's you who need work, not her. Maybe you need to work on trusting people who love you.

The phone rings. You rush to beat her to it, just in case it's Phyllis. It's not. It's Ken Fritz, one of the directors of the condominium association you belong to. You are also a director, and Ken's calling at this hour can only mean building politics.

"Ashanti," he says. He always calls you Ashanti, even though most people call you 'Shanti for short, or 'Shanteh as your buddies call you. "We have to talk," Ken continues. "We must discuss how we should vote at the board meeting tonight."

You know from experience that "how we should vote" really means "how he should vote."

"I'm so confused about the new budget Earl has proposed. I don't know whether to vote for it or not."

Ken has a reputation around the building of being very smart and very witty, a reputation that, in your opinion, he deserves. So it always surprises you that he wants your opinion on matters of condominium policies and protocol. Your recollections of Phyllis begin to fade.

"What don't you understand?" you ask.

Ken is short, probably no taller than Jean, and thin. You always thought his name should be O'Reilly or Molloy or anything Irish, because the man looks so much like a leprechaun. He is in his late fifties with a head of long, grey, Einstein-looking hair, and has grey tufts of wiry hair pushing out of his ears like the heads of grey mice.

"Well," he says, "as you know, my training is in Philosophy. I write about and teach abstract thought. I know nothing about accounting and money and business." He emphasizes the words accounting, money, and business, his already high-pitched voice growing higher on each word. "And I want to know whether or not, in your opinion, this is a good budget," he says.

He has a long thin face with heavy lines flanking his small, always-pursed mouth. It's his mouth that makes him look like a pixie. His mouth looks like a woman's mouth, as if he never opens it too wide nor stuffs big wads of bread or meat into it. He always wears a faint smile as well, and his large grey eyes always seem to sparkle when he laughs. You can almost see him smiling into the phone now.

"I don't know," you answer. "I'm no accountant, either, but . . .."

He smiles and looks sparkly-eyed even when there is nothing funny, so he often gives the impression of being amused at the people around him.

"You know, Ashanti, I wish Sean were still the president of the board."

His body language adds to his ethereal air. He walks with short, effeminate steps with his hands held away from his body like stiff lace. Jean figures he is merely gay. And in fact, you have never seen him with a woman. But you would probably be disappointed if you did, because he seems so sexless and ageless and devoid of sin.

"Sean was a good president," you say. You feel a sense of relief that the subject is off accounting.

"He was a good president," Ken repeats, "and I trusted his judgment. Sean is trained in accounting, and he knows the association's books. That Earl doesn't know what he is doing."

"A lot of people in this building would agree with you."

"I wish Sean would consider running again."

"Well," you say, "we both know how he feels about Earl and being with Earl on the board."

"Earl is such an asshole, if you'll excuse my language," he says. "He's arrogant and crass, and I think the man suffers from short-man syndrome."

"I know what you mean."

There is a pause. You begin to fidget for something to say, but he beats you to it. "What can we do to get him off the board?" he asks.

"Nothing," you answer. "The homeowners put him in. Only the homeowners can take him out."

"You certainly are filled with good news," he says. He giggles like a young girl into the phone, and you imagine little flashes of light dancing in his moth grey eyes.

You tell him which way you intend to vote on the budget, namely, against it. He thanks you and hangs up.

"So who was that?" Jean asks.

"That was Ken."

"Princess Ken?"

"One and the same," you say.

You turn back towards the bathroom, then stop.

"Don't you have to work?" you ask.

"Today is a research day," she says. "I get to breathe the dust of antiquated statutes and poorly reasoned cases 'til the library closes. So I'm in no hurry to get up. Besides, I'm hoping you'll fuck me before I have to go."

The phone rings.

"Who is it now?" she asks.

It's Earl Gilbert, president of the board.

"'Shanteh," he says, "'s up?"

"What do you want, Earl?"

Ken was right in that Earl is the quintessential pushy short man. Earl is shorter even than Ken, and has nothing of Ken's grace in movements. Earl walks like a weight-lifter or football player-- though he is neither-- shifting his weight at the shoulders with each step, and making each step hard as if to make as much noise as possible. He seems to delight in making would-be long, loping strides. But instead of evoking the image he intends, that of a rough-and-tumble cowboy, he evokes the image of a little boy imitating his father.

"I talked with Ken this morning," he says.

"You can't have talked very long," you say. "I was on the phone with him less than five minutes ago."

Earl has the kind of face at fifty that you hope you will have at fifty.

He looks as if he is thirty-eight or -nine. He has one of those faces that you imagine he hated as a teenager but loves now. It grows no hair except over his eyes, on his upper lip at the corners of his mouth, and at the very tip of his chin. The rest of his face is a smooth, even expanse of clear, clean manila folder-colored skin. No blotches, no splotches, no black-heads, no pimples. Moreover, it is completely devoid of sags and wrinkles. The corners of his eyes crinkle a little when he smiles, and the space between his eyebrows pinches a little when he frowns. But there is no evidence of these folds when he relaxes his face. The middle-aged women in the building envy him to no end. Only his hair truly reveals his age. It is a short, kinky mat that covers his head like a grey and black knit cap.

"Ken called me right after he talked to you," Earl says. "He tells me you intend to vote against my budget."

"That's right," you say. "Ken never could keep his mouth shut."

"Why must you always vote against me, 'Shanteh?"

"I'm voting against the budget, not against you."

"If you vote against my budget, you vote against me."

"That's not. . .."

"Help me, brother-man," he says. "Help me take over this board and this building."

"Earl," you say, "the . . .."

"Black folks got to stick together," he cuts you off. "Stick by me, 'Shanteh. I need your support."

He hangs up.

You are slow resting the phone back on the night stand.

"What's the matter?" Jean asks. She begins stroking your dick.

"Nothing," you answer, sitting back down on the bed. You are unsure of how to react to Earl's plea. Does he really think he could somehow take over this building? And if so, why would he even want to? Or is he merely using race to manipulate you? He has a majority of the board members in his camp without your support.

He could-- and usually does-- get anything by the board he wants. Why this plea for your vote?

Jean cuddles up to your body.

"Nothings the matter?" she asks rhetorically. She flips your limp dick from side to side with two fingers. "Nothings the matter?!" she says again in mock consternation.

"I'm sorry, honey," you say, "I . . .."

The phone rings yet again.

"That's it!" she says, "no fucky fucky this morning." She gets up and heads for the bathroom.

It's Sean Michaels.

"Hi, 'Shanti," he says. "Ken tells me that Little Caesar is at it again."

Ken is spreading pixie dust everywhere this morning.

"There are a couple of questionable line items in his proposed budget," you say.

Sean is tall though not quite as tall as you, and he is skinny, though not in the same way that Ken is skinny. Fragile is the word that best describes the way Sean looks. His face is egg-shaped, big at the top with a bulging forehead exaggerated by a receding hairline, and small at the bottom with a weak chin exaggerated by an underbite. His cheeks are flat, his eyes brown and rheumy, his teeth crooked and stained brown from smoking.

"The little bastard!" he says, "he wants to bankrupt this building."

You don't respond. You wonder if bankruptcy is part of Earl's takeover tactic.

Sean's skin is the color of sour milk, yellowish tending to green. He is in his middle thirties, but looks like the personification of sickness and impending death. He is so pale, it looks as if his skull shows through and provides the color to his skin.

"He's a little black Jew," Sean says. "He's a cheap, penny-pinching Jew. He even wears the Star of David around his neck."

The rest of his body reflects the same apparent infirmness. Some men look thin and wiry and robust. Sean looks thin and weak and sickly with blue veins visible at his temples and snaking along the backs of his hands. He even walks with a stoop.

"That's a Seal of Solomon," you correct.

"Well, it looks like a Star of David to me, and the creep lives the Jewish edict: cheap is better. Doesn't he know that you get what you pay for? When I was president of the board, I tried to upgrade the building, make it a nice place to live, increase property values. Earl has spent his entire term of office undoing the work I did. I'm surprised he hasn't torn the wallpaper off the walls in the common areas." He pauses a moment. Then he says, "I hate that little creep!"

At that moment, Jean appears in the bedroom door fully dressed.

"Listen, Sean," you say, "I've got to go."

"See you at the meeting tonight?"

"I'll be there."

You place the phone on the nightstand. "You're not leaving?" you say.

"There's certainly no reason for me to stay here."

"Aw, come on, honey," you say, "they were only a few little phone calls."

"You would rather talk condo politics with Princess Ken, King Earl and Count Dracu-Sean than stick your dick in me."

"That isn't true."

"What do you mean, 'that isn't true?'" she mimics. "Those are exactly the choices you made."

"I was being polite."

"Same thing!" she says. "I wanted your body, and you wanted to be polite."

"Honey," you say, getting off the bed and approaching her for a hug. "It isn't the way it sounds."

"It is the way it is," she says, the edge leaving her voice. "You're probably seeing someone else when you're not with me."

"Stay for breakfast," you say hugging her body, exploring the softness beneath her clothes. You could use some balm this morning after all.

"No," she says, "I'm out of the mood. We'll try again tonight after your board meeting."

She kisses you perfunctorily on the mouth, then leaves. Shit!

The room in which board meetings are conducted is located at the rear of the building on the ground floor tucked on the south side of the building between the laundry room and the rear exit. It was once two supply closets, but the first board decided it needed a permanent place in which to meet rather than relying on individual members to make their apartments available. It voted to knock out the adjoining wall, seal one of the doors, lay down a carpet, put in a dropped ceiling with recessed lights, install ventilation ducts and slap a window in the west wall. The result was an oddly shaped little office with the six concave and two convex corners that are formed when two rectangles overlap at one corner. You always thought the office was practical, but hideous. It is big enough for a small desk, two file cabinets, and one chrome and glass table with four matching chairs. Meetings were held at the table, but visitors to the meetings usually had to sit or stand along the walls or in the hallway if, as seldom was the case, a lot of homeowners attended.

Tonight, all the board members are present, Earl Gilbert, Pat Simpson, Ken Fritz, Jesus Del Lago and you. The visitors are Sean Micheals, Alice Horowitz and Maria Santos. Maybe tonight's meeting will be less boring than usual, and quickly over. After all, there is only one point of business, the budget.

"The president of the board has the power to recognize or not recognize anyone he chooses," Earl says.

"Is that power absolute?" Pat Simpson asks.

Pat Simpson is the vice president of the board, and by most accounts, a member of Earl Gilbert's camp. She is a stout, buxom woman who is always meticulously groomed, and, though not dumb, she does not grasp new concepts quickly. She always reminds you of what you thought Big Ma would be like had she married a man with money.

"Yes," Earl says, "the power is absolute."

"That isn't true," you say. "The president's power . . . .."

"Jesus has the floor," Earl says.

"The president may not use his power to thwart the expression of an elected board member," you say.

"Jesus has the floor."

You resolve at that very instant to resist any further overtures by Earl for your support. You don't like his attitude. The man obviously has nothing more than power and control on his mind, and he would use anything from friendship to fear to get it. Since he could not intimidate you-- in fact, you intimidate him with your size-- he decided to resort to the friendship approach. He must have seen the strength of your new resolve expressed in your face, because he quickly alters his position in an effort to mollify you.

"Jesus raised his hand first," Earl says. "You get the floor next."

You nod an acknowledgment.

Jesus Del Lago, treasurer, has the build of the wrestler that Earl Gilbert apparently wants to be. He is almost as tall as you are, but heavier by at least fifty pounds. The man is huge. His body looks as if it has no definition owing to the fact that it is covered with a layer of fat. The man looks like a big brown bear. Under the fat, though, there is muscle, a lot of it, because Jesus works out three-- sometimes four-- times a week with weights. Even his hands look muscular like Polish sausages tied to a ham hock.

The animal image Jesus projects is enhanced by the black, shiny, shoulder-length hair he wears parted in the middle, the fleshy brown face covered with a beard and acne, thin brown eyes that shift from person to person in the room as if he is suspicious of some wrong-doing, and the hare-lip under his shaggy mustache.

Jesus is not dumb, but he doesn't speak well. And as if he knows it and doesn't want to broadcast the fact by saying stupid things, he is laconic to a fault, and very sensitive. He would nod rather that say yes, and forced to speak, he would say as little as possible. His voice is deep, and his monosyllabic utterances sound like barks. You think he is a lot smarter than he leads people to believe. He contributes to the board meetings by asking short, concise questions that get to the crux of the issue, although he usually votes with Earl Gilbert. He rarely makes comments, and he never makes motions. He chooses tonight to make his first.

"I make a motion," Jesus says, his voice sounding like a dog growling, "that we open the floor for discussion of the new budget."

Earl shoots a look at Jesus. "You were supposed to open the discussion for board members only!"

"I second the motion," Ken says before the motion can be retracted.

"Goddamnit!" Earl says, "I don't want a whole lot of talk on this budget, I just want it passed."

"Sorry," Jesus says.

"Sorry!" Earl mimics, "sorry."

"Get off the man's case," you say.

"The man's a dummy," Earl snaps.

Jesus says nothing.

"You're a dummy, Jesus," Earl says. Earl always uses the English pronunciation of Jesus' name, so that calling him a dummy sounds like a sacrilege. Everyone in the room fidgets or groans.

"That wasn't nice," Ken says.

"I'll second that motion," Pat adds.

"It didn't mean what it sounded like it meant," Alice Horowitz says.

"I don't care how it sounded," Earl says, "I meant it, and it's true."

"You're an asshole," Jesus says.

"I'll second that motion," Alice says.

Alice Horowitz is the building's sex symbol. She is the one about whom lascivious jokes and anecdotes are whispered among the old men on the sundeck or in the laundry room. She is tall and willowy and dark-haired, and she moves with a grace that reminds you of a ballet dancer. Her legs are long and slim, and when she walks, her toes touch the ground before her heel, again like a dancer. You've seen other women walk that way, but they look phony, as if they're trying to be sophisticated when in fact they were not. Alice, by contrast, gives the impression of being sophisticated despite the phony walk.

Her face is long and thin with high, sharp cheek bones and sunken cheeks. Her lips and nose are fleshy enough to be those of a black woman, and her skin has that dark, olive, Mediterranean cast.

Jean doesn't know it, but you and Alice have a history. When you first moved into the building, the condominium board had scheduled its annual summer solstice party. It took place in one of the rooms the board rented in one of the park district mansions across the street. You went just to meet some of you neighbors. Alice was there; Jean was not. You mingled and met a few people. Finally, you introduced yourself to Alice. She had been sitting on one of the leather sofas talking with one of the building's elderly couples for about an hour before they decided it was time for them to get back in. When they got up to leave, Alice looked at you and pretended not to see you. You forced the issue.

"Hi," you had said sticking your hand out, "my name is Ashanti. What's your's."

She told you her name. "Alice," she whispered. She blinked her eyes slowly. And for the first time, you realized she was drunk. Not sloppy, but drunk none the less. You told her you were new in the building; she said she had been there for five years. You talked for another fifteen minutes. Then she said, "Ashanti, I hardly know you, but I need your help."

Wanting to give the impression of being a gentleman, you answered, "anything, anything at all."

"I'm drunk," she said, "and I need someone to walk me back to the building. I'm afraid to cross Sheridan Road alone."

"Sure," you said, "let's go."

You stood up, and she struggled to get her equilibrium. With your help, she stood up and held your arm tightly. You walked her home. In the lobby, you were going to put her in the elevator, and head back across the street, but she insisted that you see her to the door. You went up with her. She fumbled for her keys, unlocked the door, then stumbled inside and fell flat on the floor.

"Damn," you said. "Damn."

She lifted her arm for you to help her, so you pulled her to her feet, and she collapsed in your arms. You closed the door with one foot and dragged her into her bedroom. You plopped her on the bed. She rolled into a wobbly sitting position. "Help me with my shoes," she said. "I am so drunk!"

You were reluctant to get too close to her. You never know how she might react, but you untied the laces and took her shoes off.

"Rub my feet," she said.

So much for not getting too close. Still you decided to use a clinical approach, like a professional masseuse. You began to massage her feet, and she began to moan. You stopped.

"Don't stop," she said, "I like it."

Was this woman trying to set you up? You rubbed her feet, then her calves. You could smell that her pussy was getting wet. You stopped rubbing. She wiggled her foot as a signal for you to keep going. If this was a setup, you were hooked. You rubbed her calves again, but not to massage them. This time you rubbed them to arouse her. Her stockings were in the way. You watched for her reaction as you reached under her dress to remove her pantyhose. She lay still, her breathing bordered on snoring. Now *you* were aroused. You grabbed the waistband of her pantyhose at her sides, and dragged it down. Her panties came down, too. The scent of her pussy was strong. You breathed in deeply, and felt your pulse increase. You stood back and pulled them all the way down to her feet. In her sleep, she began to work them off with her toes. You saved her the trouble by pulling them the rest of the way off for her. Your dick began to swell. She cradled a pillow under her neck as she turned over onto her side, and opened her legs as far as she could get them. She had surprisingly little pubic hair, and you could see the pink, turkey neck-like skin that formed the lips of her pussy. By now, your dick was all the way hard. You settled yourself on your knees between her gapped legs, and began rubbing her calves again, one with each hand. She sighed. You moved up to her thighs and rubbed them slowly but firmly, her creamy white skin soft and smooth under your hands. With every breath, she sighed slowly. You moved your hands up to her butt and rubbed with the same slow firm motion. Her butt was more firm than you would have expected. She took a breath, and held it. With one hand, you scratched the thin clump of dark hair around her pussy. Her body began to quiver gently. You separated her lips, and her breath began to quiver as well. You stroked her clitoris. She let out a long, even sigh. She was so wet, it was easy to slide your middle, ring and pinkie fingers into her pussy as far as they would go. She buried her face in that pillow and groaned deep in her throat as she came. With your other hand, you unbuttoned and unzipped your pants, and pushed them down around your ankles. Feeling you nestling up behind her, she pulled herself to her knees, arched her back, and, using both hands, spread her lips apart. You pushed your dick into her. She murmured, "Oh, my God," under her breath. It was as if she didn't believe it. It struck you as a strange response. What didn't she believe? The bigness? The smallness? Its existence? Its existence in her? She was tight as if she hadn't done this in a long time. You had to push three times in order for it to go in as far as it would go. You pushed against the bottom of her pussy a few times, and she came again. This time, she mewed like a kitten. Finally, she said, "Don't come inside me there."

"Where do you want it?"

"Where ever *you* want it."

"In the back."

You pulled it out, and moved it up an inch careful to drag as much fluid from her pussy as you could. There was more resistance this time, but she stiffened her body to allow you to push it all the way in. This time it took closer to ten pushes to get comfortable.

Suddenly, you felt a kinship with this woman, this Alice. She was just like you imagined yourself to be. She was honest. This was a woman who loved to fuck. Well, so did Jean, with those little worker hands of hers. But Alice was different. Alice was an artist. You imagined that she was the kind of woman who would call herself a whore and be proud of it. She knew the power she held in her pussy, the strength, the wisdom, the courage, and she drew on it. She drew from her pussy the way grass and trees and lilies drew from the sun, or the way you drew from your name. Women like her were rare. She was like a comet that whirls around the earth every hundred and fifty years. Those who are living when it passes feel special. Those who know that it will never pass during their lifetime feel deprived. Alice made you feel special.

As you pushed in and out of her rectum, she rubbed her hand in and out of her pussy. She began to come before you did, and the sensation must have been intense, because her body quaked for what seemed like five full minutes before the itch began to rise in you. You held it back for as long as you could. By the time you came, she was chanting "oh" like a mantra. "Oh, oh, oh, oh, oh." You had never seen a woman come so deeply. Only special women can come like that. When she was done, her hand was covered with fluid from her pussy. She slumped to her side, pulling your dick out of her ass. You rolled beside her on your back. She put her hand on your chest. You could smell the pussy on her fingers. You put her index finger in your mouth and sucked it, then her middle finger, then her ring finger, then her pinkie. Her come had a delicate, salty taste.

You got up and dressed yourself, and went to the bathroom to pee. When you got back, she was curled under the covers. You sat on the side of the bed.

"Can you see yourself out?" she asked.

Her back was to you as she spoke. You reached your hand under the cover and rubbed her ass one more time. The crack was still wet. You pushed your finger into her rectum and rotated it around the rim a few times.

"I can see myself out," you said. "Will I see you again?" You chuckled at the banality of the question.

She snored loudly. This time she was asleep for real.

The next morning, she was on the elevator as you were going down to work. She was wearing dark sunglasses and a wide straw hat. There were only the two of you there.

"Hi, Alice," you said.

She didn't answer. The elevator stopped at the ground floor, and she bolted off on her way to the bus stop. She didn't even look back. That was three years ago.

Since then, you have seen her only in passing. She didn't attend any more of the building's summer solstice parties, and though she did attend monthly board meetings, she always managed to avoid looking at you. By contrast, you always struggled to keep you eyes off of her.

Tonight is no different. Her hair looks a little rumpled on the sides because she has a habit of fingering her hair during conversations. She fingers it now as she turns her attention to Earl Gilbert.

"You have no right to address people in such a vile tone."

"Shut up," Earl says. "Just shut up." He pauses a moment, then says,

"This meeting is over."

He looks at you as if for support. You look him straight in the eye, and give him nothing.

"I said this meeting is over!"

No one moves. Earl stands up abruptly, the blood in his face rising. "The board is going to pay for this," he hisses through clinched teeth. "I am going to sue your asses off."

"You've got no grounds for anything even resembling a lawsuit," you snap.

"You're undermining the power of the presidency."

"You are acting beyond the scope of your power."

"What is the scope of his power," Maria Santos asks.

"The president controls the board," Earl blurts.

"Wrong! " you say, "the president carries out the mandate of the board."

"The president is the chief executive officer, and presides over the board," Earl says.

"He presides over board meetings," you counter.

"Damn you, 'Shanti," Earl says, "I am going to get you for this."

"Don't fuck with me, little man," you snarl. "You don't weigh enough."

You look straight into his eyes as you speak. After a short moment, he turns and pushes his way by Sean Micheals who is standing in the doorway.

"Uppity little thing, ain't he?" Pat says.

"He's an arrogant little prick," Sean says.

Ken smiles ethereally, and Jesus sits grinding his teeth. You turn your head, and look directly at Alice. She looks you in the eye with a faint smile on her face. Then she abruptly looks away. "So what do we do now?" she asks.

"Actually," you say, "Earl is right. This meeting is over."

"You don't have to leave just because his shortness leaked out," Sean snaps.

"We are here to vote on a budget," you say.

"But Earl didn't present a budget," Pat whines.

"'Shanti's point exactly," Maria counters.

Ken glances around the room at each of us, then says, "I motion that we adjourn the meeting." His voice sounds light and airy.

"Second," Jesus says.

You have the distinct feeling that Jesus, more than anyone else present, relishes the idea of not having to sit through a meeting where Earl prances around spitting insults for sport.

You vote, and the meeting ends. Under the guise of straightening the place up, you linger in the office as the other people leave. You want to be able to watch Alice to see if she looks at you again. She doesn't. You watch as she follows the others to the elevator. A long moment passes, and the elevator doors open. Just before she steps in, she turns her gaze directly on you. With no particular expression on her face, she holds the glance eye to eye for a split second longer than she has to, then looks down as she steps on. You finish up in the office and head upstairs to your apartment.

You consider calling Alice. But then you remember that you have never had her phone number. Ships passing in the night have no need to signal one another. You call Jean, but there is no answer. Then you remember that she is going to be at the library until late. "Breathing the dust of antiquated statutes and poorly reasoned cases" were her words. Phyllis comes to mind, the smell of his skin next to your face. No way! You feel deceived like an insect that has been lured by the call of mate only to discover the call was being imitated by a predator, a praying mantis in a short black dress. All of a sudden, you can smell the oil he used to lubricate his butt, and the fact that you find the remembrance pleasant pisses you off. You vow never to see him again.

What about the Latin Club again? You decide to go to a movie. After calling the Village and "400" theaters, you decide to go to the "400." You just aren't up for the cheaply produced martial arts movies at the Village. It's the dubbing. You aren't up for watching some silk-clad grand master of Kung Fu in a Hong Kong death temple mouthing the Gettysburg address while you are hearing the words "kill him." You opt for the latest science fiction thriller about a computer programmer saving mankind through the use of mathematical and artistic genius. Being a programmer, you like movies that portray programmers and programming in a thaumaturgical light. Lawyers and doctors and cops probably get the same charge you do watching actors glorifying their lives. After the movie, you decide to get some grapes and pears and brie. Your plan is to have incense burning and soft music playing when Jean stops by from the library. From the store, you go into the back of the building and by the little misshapen building office. The light is on, and Earl is looking through some files.

You poke your head in. "Need any help?"

"Not from you, I don't," Earl snarls.

"Brother-man, ..."

"Brother-man?!" He cuts you off, "Now it's brother-man! Where were you at the meeting when I needed your support?"

"You were wrong," you say.

"Fuck wrong!" he says, "I'm black, and that's what counts."

You look at him. His young-looking face appears hard with tension, his lips pinched, his jaw muscles and eyebrows tight under his smooth, creamy skin. You pity him. They say that the first step to wisdom is to know that you don't know. Earl spent large portions of his life trying to compensate with his actions for what he lacked in stature. But he didn't have to. Nobody cared that he was short. He had other qualities. He was intelligent, articulate, even witty when he wasn't being caustic. Then there was that smooth skin that we all envied. The trouble is, he didn't know. Worst, he didn't know that he didn't know. "Being black," you say measuring your voice, "does not excuse acting a fool."

"Fuck you, you big tub of Oreo shit! And get the fuck out of here."

You close the door as you leave. You can hear him screaming through the door. "You are a disgrace to the race," he says. You take the elevator to the fifteenth floor.

There is a message from Jean on your answering machine saying that she is home and wants to see your body. You put the fruit and cheese on a plate to warm, light the incense, then call her.

"You're in luck," you say. "My body has just informed me that it wants to be seen by only you."

"Ha! Any pussy would do. Mine just happens to be handy."

"Not so," you protest.

"And just how did it inform you?"

"It raised a flagpole as a signal."

She laughs, and says she will be right up.

Jean has a one-bedroom apartment on seven on the west side of the building. You know she will be at your house in a minute or two at the most, so you head for the kitchen to cut the cheese.

Maybe she was more honest than you gave her credit for. At least she had the courage to make her distrust of you known. She knew you could not be faithful despite the fact that not just any pussy would do, and she was willing to face it.

Certainly, there *were* other pussies that would do nicely, and at least once, there was a not-pussy that did for the short term. You could smell Phyllis' oil again. Just then, the phone rings. You expect it to be Jean.

"I know," you say without saying hello. "You're wondering what kind of flag to run up my pole."

There is a pause. Then a voice whispers, "Come down to the office."

"Earl?" you say. "Is that you?"

The connection breaks. After a couple of moments, you hear a dial tone.

You stand there for what seems like a full minute. What is with this cloak and dagger shit? Jean knocks on the door.

"Listen," you say letting her in, "cut the cheese that's in the kitchen, and open some wine. I've got to run down to the office."

"What's the matter?" she asks

"I don't know."

As you approach the door to the office, you see that it is ajar and that the light is out. You wonder what kind of trick Earl is planning. You are in no mood for games, so you shove the door hard. It hits the wall and bounces back towards you. You stop it with your foot. Even with the lights off, you can see Earl sitting at the desk resting face down as if he were taking a nap.

"Earl," you call, "what's the problem?"

You turn the light on, and see the small pool of blood under his head. Blood covers his hands and lap like spilled soup. Blood runs in a thin stream down the front of the desk and forms a pool at one leg of the chair.

You hear yourself gasp, "Oh, my God!"

Just then, Maria Santos walks up. She looks at you and smiles a greeting. She is about to speak when she sees Earl. She screams. Then she looks at you and screams even louder.

Maria Santos is fat, and most of her fat is on the upper half of her body. She looks like a pear resting on its stem. She has huge breasts, wide, rounded shoulders and thick, fleshy biceps. Her mid-rift protrudes over her belt, but his hips and behind are flat, almost masculine. Her legs are skinny; her feet are flat, and her toes splay out as if she were forcing them apart. You wonder how she manages to put shoes on.

Her face is fleshy like the rest of her upper body. She has a double chin, thick ruddy cheeks, and narrow eyes that look as if they are difficult to open because of the heavy lids over them. Her hair is black and silky and grows down past her butt.

Her voice as she screams is high and shrill like a jungle cat. You reach out to touch her, to calm her, but she cringes and backs away from you. She turns and bolts two at a time up the stairs across from the rear elevator. Her screams in the stairwell resonate and echo. You can hear her until she reaches the floor she lives on and closes the stairwell door behind her.

"Damn," you say aloud. You know she thinks you are responsible for Earl's death, and you begin to wonder about an alibi. You check your watch. It is midnight. You have only been here about two minutes, and Jean can corroborate your story.

Just then, you feel a hand on your shoulder. You turn half expecting Earl to be standing there wiping actors' make-up off his face. Instead, it is Ken Fritz smiling up at you with wide-eyed wonder like a yogi in a state of bliss.

"Ken," you say, "I thought you were Earl."

He laughs like a teenage girl in some guy's back seat. "Heaven forbid," he says, hunching up his shoulders.

"What I meant was . . .." You begin to realize how difficult it will be to explain that you thought he was Earl because Earl looks dead and you want Earl to be alive because Maria Santos thinks you are the killer and because you don't want a murder to happen in your building and because you think it was Earl's voice on the phone a few minutes ago and that you were alone in this corridor except for Earl face down at the desk. You look over at the office. The door is tightly closed, although you don't remember closing it. You decide not to explain. Instead, you say, "We must call the police."

Ken's smile fades, and he looks away.

"Earl has been killed," you continue, "and I'm afraid Maria thinks I did it."

You wait at the front of the building as the police and ambulance arrive. The paramedics rush in, and within minutes, they load Earl's body into the back of the ambulance. Strangely, his face isn't covered.

People in America are no longer accustomed to death, natural death. These days, death is ritualized with the accouterments of medical paraphernalia. Bottles of fluids, masks, gauges, shiny steel instruments. That's what hospitals are for. That's what doctors do. They minister in death. When we see the white frocks, those damned white frocks, it's like the mafia kiss of death. Somebody always dies. And since we know that death can happen, we prepare ourselves. Otherwise, we don't see death in our natural surroundings except by accident. And we have come to think of death as an accident, something that is not supposed to happen. Something that is foreign, alien, out of the ordinary. So when it comes, we are unprepared. We are shocked. We gossip about it in small groups. We watch its custodians clean up after it. We listen as its chroniclers and pundits try to figure it out, to assess and assign blame. One of its minions, a uniformed police officer, beckons you back inside to answer some questions.

Detective Arnold Middleman looks like the caricature of an aging Hollywood actor. Having set eyes on the man for the very first time, you know that you don't like him. He is a little taller than Jean, and he has a round stomach and thick limbs like W. C. Fields. Maybe thats why you don't like him. You never liked W. C. Fields. His face looks like an infant's face, round and fat with blue eyes and dimples and red patches that look like the marks left by someone who has just pinched his cheeks. He looks a lot more like Mickey Rooney than W.C. Fields. But you never liked Mickey Rooney, either. He wears an ill-fitting toupee that is two shades darker than the hair over his ears, and when he smiles, all of his teeth shine. His smile looks mechanical like the forced smiles of beauty pageant contestants, and his gestures are overly broad like those of a poorly portrayed Shakespearean character. Everything about the man strikes you as phoney.

"His throat," he pauses as if waiting for the dramatic tension to peak before delivering the rest of his line, "has been cut." He places extra emphasis on the word "cut" so that it snaps out of his mouth like a seed from a ruptured pod.

"Who found him?" he asks.

The hallway outside the building office is crowded with on-lookers waiting for details of the incident. They also serve as an audience for Middleman's histrionics.

"I did," you answer.

"Mack," he says to the officer, "get the names and numbers of these good people, and send them home. You, sir," he says to you," shall speak to me now."

He bids you to follow him through the on-lookers and into the laundry room where there are a card table and two chairs set up as if for a game of poker. He sits on one side of the table with his back to the wall so that he can keep his eye on the entrance. You sit facing him. "What's your name?"

You tell him. He jots it down on a yellow notepad.

"You live in this building?"

"I own a condo here, and I'm a board member."

"You're on the board of directors?" He looks surprised. You know it is because you are black, and the asshole can't believe a black man could be elected to the board of directors of a North Sheridan Road condominium.

"Yes, and a past president."

"Ok," he says, "Tell me what you know."

Even his voice grates on you. You tell him about the phone call and what you saw upon entering the office. You also tell him about Maria Santos and Ken Fritz. He writes their names down, too.

"I won't know for sure," he says, "until he has been examined, but it appears that this incident happened at least an hour ago."

"An hour ago," you say looking at your watch, "would be eleven-thirty. At that time, I was just getting in from a movie. Earl was healthy at that time, because I saw him looking through the office files."

"You saw him at eleven-thirty, and found him bleeding at midnight, is that correct?"

"That's right," you say. You want this interview to be over so you can get out of the man's space.

"And you came down at midnight because of a phone call?"

"Right, again," you say.

"And between eleven-thirty and twelve, you were . . .." He pauses waiting for you to fill in the rest.

". . . in my apartment chilling wine and warming cheese."

"Alone?"

"Yes, until just before I came downstairs and found him."

"Until eleven-fifty-five," he says.

"Yes."

He pauses a moment, then says, "I'd like for you to come down to the station to make a statement about finding the body and all."

"A statement?"

"Yeah, it's routine, just some paperwork we have to complete."

"Why can't we do it here?"

"I don't have my secretary here, and all the forms we need are there. It'll only take a few minutes."

You could certainly tell he is an actor. All of a sudden, he has this beatific smile as if everything was going to be just fine. As if there were no murder and all was right with the world. "I'll get my shoes," you say.

Jean is asleep on the sofa. The television is tuned to CNN. She wakes up as you walk in. "What took you so long?" she asks, rubbing her eyes with the knuckles of the index fingers.

"Earl's been murdered."

"What?" She is fully awake now and animated. Her eyes are blinking in disbelief.

"They want me to go to the station to make a statement."

"Don't do it," she says. Now she is more than fully awake. She is on high alert.

"Why not?"

"Have they arrested you?"

"No."

"I'm going with you."

"You don't have to do that."

"This isn't a courtesy offer," she says. Her voice is hard, harder than you have ever heard it before. "You are in deep shit."

"Why? I didn't do anything."

She stands up and moves directly in front of you. It looks like she's about to start a fight. "Listen, 'Shanti," she says, "I'm a lawyer. I deal with these asshole cops every day." She pokes the air to accentuate 'every day,' one poke per word. 'Day' gets an especially hard poke. "This is not about a statement about finding a body. They want to interrogate you. They want to make you confess."

"I won't confess to something I didn't do, and I didn't do anything."

"Trust me," she said, "These people are not to be toyed with. Don't say anything to them without me being there with you." She heads for the front door. "Wait here while I go get dressed."

Shit! The last thing you need is to be coming to the police station with a woman. Fuck that. You slip on your shoes, and head downstairs.

Middleman smiles as you leave the elevator. "I really appreciate you helping us like this. My name is Arnold, by the way."

He leads you to a waiting unmarked car in the driveway. He opens the door for you, and you scoot into the back seat. He gets in next to the driver, a ruddy-faced man with close-cut blond hair. He looks like a poster boy for the Marines. The driver eases the car away. Just then, Jean dashes from the front elevator and bolts out of the lobby door obviously trying to catch you.

"Who is that?" Middleman asks.

"She's my lawyer."

Middleman's expression changes. His eyes look alert like those of a fox that has just caught scent of a wolf. The driver punches the gas, and the car squeals out of the driveway. Middleman puts on his beatific smile again. "So what do you do, Ashanti?"

"Well, Detective, . . ."

"Call me Arnie."

"Ok, Arnie, I program computers."

"Oh? Where at?"

"One of the big banks downtown."

"You must make a lot of money."

"I do all right."

"More than cops."

"I don't know what cops make."

"Not enough for a gold-capped tooth."

You arrive at the station, and they lead you in through a side door and through a short corridor that leads into an open office with lots of desks. They lead you to a small conference room off to the side. Middleman opens the door and bids you to enter. "Can I get you some coffee?"

"None for me, thanks. I plan to be going to bed as soon as I get back."

"I'll be back in a minute," he says, and closes the door.

The room is pale green and well lit. The table and chairs look like U.S. government issue, grey steel with dark green vinyl. You pick a chair on the far side of the table facing the door and sit. You look around for a clock. There isn't one. You fold your arms across your chest and try to guess how late it might be. It must be at least one in the morning.

The sound of the door latch wakes you up. You have that waking-up-on-a-bus feeling, and look around to see where you are. Middleman walks in with the poster boy who drove the car. Middleman pulls out a chair and slides it next to you. The poster boy stands across the table with his hands on his hips. In this light, he looks surprisingly like a male version of Jean. Pale skin, thin, chiseled lips. They could almost be from the same tribe. Middleman leans forward, rests his elbows on his knees like he's about to confide a secret. He sighs. "Jack here thinks you did it."

Disbelief comes in many forms. There is mild disbelief like the time Big Ma found all those empty candy wrappers in the garbage, and you and Janet stood there and said you didn't eat them. She suspected you were lying, but maybe somebody else did it. Her disbelief was mild. There is medium disbelief like the first time you made love to Jean. You couldn't believe your dry spell was finally over. You must have popped in her four times that night just to prove it was true. There is high disbelief like the look in Jean's eyes when you told her Earl had been murdered. That's the no-it-can't-be level. Then there is the pigs-can-fly level of disbelief. This is the nothing-on-the-face-of-the-earth-can-make-you-believe-it level of disbelief. You stand bolt upright, "What?!" Your chair goes flying over.

"Take it easy," Middleman says retrieving the chair for you. "We can work this out."

"There is nothing to work out! I didn't do it!" You look over at Jack.

Jack says, "You're going down on this one, big boy."

"Excuse me!"

"You heard me. I'm taking you down."

"But I didn't do it!"

"And your point?"

"Fuck you!"

"No, fuck you. I'm taking your black nigger ass down."

You step around ready to go to jail for breaking a cops nose when

Middleman jumps between you. He has a hand on your chest and a hand on Jack's chest. "Get out of here, Jack! You are way out of line."

"Remember what I said." Jack spits the words over his shoulder as he leaves.

You can hear your pulse beating in your ears. "I'm gon' kick that bastard's ass."

Middleman sits down, and gestures for you to do the same. "C'mon, Ashanti, sit down."

You sit down, but you are not relaxed. "What the fuck is going on here?" you ask. "I thought I was here to make some kind of statement about finding the body."

Middleman leans forward again, just like before. He sighs, just like before. "We need you to make a confession."

"Hell no! And fuck you, too."

"I'm trying to help you here."

"You never told me I was under arrest."

"Yeah, we did."

"You never read me my Miranda rights."

"Yeah, we did. You just don't remember."

Then you do remember. Jean said don't answer any questions without her being there. "I want my lawyer," you say.

"Aw, c'mon, Ashanti," Middleman says. "We've got you dead to rights. You're just going to make it harder on yourself."

"I want my fucking lawyer."

"We know you did it."

Jean was right. You *are* in deep shit.

"Am I going to have to bring Jack back in here? He doesn't like you, and he might get rough."

He looks at you looking back at him. "Ok," he says. "You leave me no choice."

He sighs deeply, stands up histrionically, and leaves.

You expect Jack to come bounding in, but he doesn't. In fact, nothing at all happens. You sit, and you wait. You wonder how close it is to daylight.

You're awakened again by the sound of the door latch. This time, though, you stand up ready to fight, but it's still not Jack. It's a young kid in an ill-fitting grey suit. He looks like he barely shaves. "Hi," he says extending his hand. "My name is McCorkle. Tim McCorkle. I represent the people, and I'm here to help you."

"Where's Ms. Dobson."

"Who is that?"

"Jean Dobson. She's my attorney."

"She's not here. I'm going to be helping you."

"Then get me the fuck out of here."

"Well, first I need to ask you some questions."

"Like what?"

"Like did you and the victim have an argument or something?"

"We passed some words at a board meeting, but it didn't rise to the level of an argument. What has that got to do with this?"

"Had you ever threatened him?"

"No, but so what? Get me out of here!"

"Mr. Ra, I'm trying to help you. Do you own a pocket knife or a straight razor?"

"No! Now, are you going to get me out of here or not?"

The door opens. Jack walks in. He's followed by another cop, a black cop with large hands and feet like a teenager. "That's ok, Tim, we'll take it from here."

"Sorry, guys," Tim says, "he just didn't fall for it." Tim gives you a cat-who-ate-the-canary look as he leaves closing the door behind him.

"Ok, big man," Jack says, "now we're going to do it my way. I want a confession. I want it now."

"I didn't do it."

"Maybe I didn't make myself clear. I want a confession, and I want it now."

"Fuck you."

Jack step forward and throws a right cross. You duck and try to throw a right hook, but the other cop grabs your arm. The two of them wrestle you to the floor. Jack rears back to punch you in the face while you're down, and the door opens again. A Sargent walks in. "Have you got an Ashanti Ra in here," he says.

"Yeah, we got him," Jack says.

"Let him up," the Sargent says. "His lawyer is here with an I-bond."

"You haven't seen the last of me," Jack says as he backs off you. "This is only the beginning."

On the drive home, Jean is nobly restrained. She doesn't utter a single I-told-you-so. It's already late afternoon. They kept you there for over twelve hours.

"Ok, counselor," you say. "What's next?"

"You get some sleep. I've got some leg work to do."

"What do people without lawyers do?" you ask.

"They go to jail."

"Even if they didn't do it?"

"Even if they didn't do it."

You get home and plop straight into bed. The dream you have seems to be an extension of the day. It begins with loud, hysterical screams from someplace outside your field of vision. You know they are Maria's screams, but it is not Maria's voice. The voice is more shrill, yet more gravelly. There is a mechanical quality to it as well like the voice from a supermarket cash register. The timbre of the voice grates on your nerves, and you can feel yourself turning uneasily in your sleep. The next morning, despite the fact that you force yourself to stay in bed longer than normal, you feel tired.

You shower and eat eggs and toast. As you sip the last of your orange juice, you turn the other day's events over in your mind. Home at eleven-thirty. Offer to help Earl. Mystery call at eleven-fifty-five. You try to remember the voice. Muffled. Whispery. Instructions to come down to the office. What made you think the voice was Earl's? Could you be sure the voice was a man's? You conclude that you could, but to conclude that it was Earl's requires a leap of existential proportions. Obviously, someone is trying to pin this murder on you. But who? And aside from saving their own neck, why? Why pick you as the scapegoat? You try to think of whom your enemies in the building might be. You could think of no one with whom you get along more poorly than Earl. Shit! Why couldn't it have been someone outside the building?! This could have been a routine burglary.

The phone rings. It's Jean. "You've got to leave!"

"Why?" you ask.

"They're coming to arrest you."

"What?!"

"I'm at the station now. That asshole McCorkle went before Judge Snow and told him about the fight you had with the police yesterday. He got him to revoke you bond and to issue a warrant for your arrest."

"*They* were kicking *my* ass!"

"The warrant is for the incident in the building."

"But I didn't do it."

"They don't care who did it," she says, "they care about arresting somebody. They care about arresting you."

"But I . . .."

"Goddamnit, 'Shanti, leave before it is too late." She hangs up the phone.

Shit! Jean was right. You had to leave. You throw on some jeans and a T-shirt. You grab your wallet, your bank book and your keys. Leave the radio on and the door unlocked. Make it look like you'll be back in a minute or two. From the front window, you see a police car pulling into the driveway. You avoid the elevator and take the stairs. Just as you get to the third floor, the door to the stairwell flings open. It's Jesus. He's deep in thought, and nearly runs into you. He stops short. "Sorry," he says, stepping to his left just as you step to the right. Your reflexes are synchronized. He steps to the right just as you step to the left. Finally, you both stop, almost nose to nose. He is embarrassed, and barks a single syllable laugh, "Ha!"

You are anxious to jump by, but you want to appear calm. "Jesus," you say, "how you doing?"

"'Shanti," he says. "I'm so glad I ran into you." He picks now to string more than three words together. "I need to talk to you, man."

"Oh, about what?" You resist the urge to bolt.

"I know you can help me 'cause everybody know you the man with the ladies, man."

"What do you need?"

"I need advice. There's this girl, and I don't know what to do."

You listen as doors up and down the stairwell open and close. "Do I know her?"

"It's Maria, man. I love her, and I think she love me."

You hear in your head the scream she let out last night, and the urge to escape grows. You reach into your pocket and begin turning your car keys between your fingers. "Have you said anything to her?"

"No, man, I'm scared."

He's scared! "Scared of what?"

"She might not like me." You never noticed it before, but Jesus has eyes like a cow, big and brown. He looks at you, then at the floor, then at you again. "What if she don't like me."

"What if she does?"

"She a nurse, man, over at County Hospital. I'm just a laborer."

Your anxiety mounts. "Talk to her."

"What should I say?"

"The worst that can happen is that she says no." You can feel yourself inching along the railing to move on.

He sees you sliding away, but ignores it. "You right, man. I talk to her. I talk to her today." He turns abruptly and exits the stairwell.

Your anxiety is near panic. You take the rest of the stairs down two at a time. You get in the car, and turn the key. The starter whirs, but the engine only coughs. "Shit!" You turn it again, and the car starts. You back out of the stall, and hit the button to open the garage door. The police car is still parked in the driveway. Jack is in it, but he is busy writing on something in his lap. Middleman must be inside. Your stomach is churning. You pull quickly up the ramp, hoping the tint on your rear windows will shield you from his view. You head south on Sheridan Road to the Outer Drive.

What now? Where do you go? What do you do? Who do you call? You can't go home. You can't go to any friends' house, because the police will contact all of them. You can't contact relatives for the same reason. It's unfortunate how we have come to rely so heavily on the social infrastructure. People aren't people anymore. Free. Autonomous. We're cells in a body. We go where the body wants us to go. And which cells form the brains of this body? The government? The President? Suppose the muscles and blood and bones don't want to go where the brain wants to go. Should they revolt? *Can* they revolt? What does revolt even mean?

You pull off the Drive and head west. The driver in a dull grey Ford with shiny new chrome wheels cuts you off. You jam the brakes to avoid hitting him. Asshole! You can hear the loud, rhythmic bass line of the hip-hop music playing inside. Boom, boom-boom, boom, boom-boom. The music is so loud, the speakers rattle. Four young brothers bounce in their seats to the sounds. You're pissed off, and you want to get around them. They're doing the speed limit. You can't afford to draw the attention of police, so you pull back, and cruise behind them. Boom, boom-boom, boom, boom-boom. Their music is annoying, and you wonder how they can stand the volume.

They cruise through the intersection at Clark street. Boom, boom-boom, boom, boom-boom. The light is green. You follow them. A police car pulls behind you from off of Clark. Oh, shit! You check your speed. Thirty miles per hour. They don't know your car, so they can't know to stop you. You can feel the heat rising from your collar. Boom, boom-boom, boom, boom-boom. They turn the blue lights on. Damn! What are you going to say? Should you make a break? No. Just chill. See what they want. Boom, boom-boom, boom, boom-boom. They beep the siren. You pull over. Your stomach is churning. They pull around. One of them gets on the bullhorn, "Pull over grey Ford." Your sense of relief is palpable. The music is stopped.

With relief comes safety. With safety comes complacency. Why were the cops stopping the Ford? They weren't speeding. There were no malfunctioning lights on the car. With complacency comes carelessness. You pull into a parking space two car lengths behind the cops, and you watch. The first cop, the driver, gets out and walks to the Ford. The second cop positions himself behind the Ford as cover for the first cop. He can see everything that is going on, but the folks in the Ford don't even know he's there. This is a military operation. The first cop orders everybody out of the car. The brothers grouse and grumble, but they get out. All four of them are wearing baggy pants that hang half off their asses, and unlaced gym shoes. The cop in the back takes charge of the brothers exiting on the passenger side. Both cops order the brothers to get spread eagle on the Ford. More grousing. More grumbling. They comply. The cops pat them down. Then the cops begin digging in the brothers' pockets, taking out their wallets, going through their wallets and papers. One cop, the first one, takes some papers out, balls them up, and throws them on the ground. He stuffs the wallet back into somebody's pocket.

After the pat-down, the brothers are ordered to wait on the sidewalk. The second cop stands guard over them while the first cop searches the car. He empties the glove compartment and the trunk. He searches under the seats. He strews candy and potato chip bags into the street along with straws and half-finished cups of pop. All the doors are open. Then he looks over at you and does a double take. Do all cops have that poster boy look? They must affect that. He orders the brothers back into the Ford. Then to you, he asks, "What the fuck are you looking at?"

"Nothing, officer," you answer, "I just had to stop to fasten my seatbelt." You put the car in gear and pull away.

You cruise over to Western Avenue, and turn south. The longest street in Chicago. It'll take you a little while to get to the other end. You know there's only one place you can go. Just not yet.

IV

They say that family deaths occur in sets of three. Collis was number one. Your parents were numbers two and three in a fiery crash in the Pyrenees Mountains in the south of France about a month later.

Big Ma had been crying buckets over Collis. "My baby," she would moan, "my baby is dead." Reggie tried to console her as much as he could. "You still got me, mama," he told her. She hugged him and cried the more. Reggie hardly cried at all, because it was Collis she was missing.

The news of your parents' deaths changed her. She still cried, but it was a different kind of cry. Now she cried because she realized how selfish she had been.

The call came on a Saturday morning. Big Ma answered the phone, then tilted her head and put a finger in her other ear in order to block out the surrounding noise. After a long silence, she gasped and put her hand over her mouth. She looked directly at me for a long moment. Then she looked at Janet. Tears began to well up in her eyes as she squeezed them shut and hung up the phone.

"Dear sweet Jesus," she said, "you babies is all alone." Then she heaved a great sigh. "Y'all gon' live with me. That's what Collis would have wanted. Y'all gon' live with me."

You look over at Reggie staring at you from just beyond the door to his room. His eyes narrow to thin slits, and he forces his lips tight together. He reminds you of the man you and Collis had seen dragging the trunk. His stare is at you and, at the same time, through you as if he is looking far off at some distant loathing. You can feel a tightness growing in your chest.

Since you and Janet were already staying with Big Ma while your parents were in Europe for a couple of months, the change to simply staying with Big Ma was a simple one, you and Janet stopped talking about going home. This was it. This was home now. So when Jame and Li'l Bo left, you stayed. Naturally, they thought staying with Big Ma all the time was great. This was where all the fun things in the world happened. They couldn't know about the not-so-fun things that happened there. Reggie said he would poke your eyes out if you told anyone anything about what he was doing to you. Worst of all, he threatened to poke Janet's eyes out.

"You little punk," Reggie said to you. "If you don't bend over, ah'm gon' poke her eyes out, and then ah'm gon' kill her just like that man killed Collis. And ain't nobody never gon' find out about it."

So you would bend over and Reggie would push himself into you and you would squirm. "Be still," he would bark, "I ain't through yet." He would hug you tightly, but not so tightly that he hurt you. The hugs felt warm. Then he would groan and you would feel the pressure inside you relax. That's when he would push you away. "Get away from me you little punk."

Sometimes you would bleed, and the pain would be so bad that you would beg him to use some Vaseline. "Yeah, get some grease, you little bitch. And you can put some on your mouth." You did what he said, and you swallowed when he said swallow. "And you bet' not tell mama, either."

You were ten years old when Big Ma, Reggie, Janet and you moved to the west side. It was in the fall. You lived on the first floor. The space under the stairs to the second floor created a closet and storage room in your front hallway. The thing about this closet was that it assumed a different character depending on the light. In the morning, it was harmless. Sometimes the door would be ajar, and the light of day would slice in revealing out-of-season clothes, Christmas ornaments, luggage and run-over shoes. In the evening, the light would change and sometimes play tricks on you. The out-of-season clothes would look like a man hunched over trying to conceal himself. The luggage could look like dogs or toads or the scaly back of the creature from the Black Lagoon. At night, you wouldn't even look that way. In fact, you avoided that hallway altogether. At night, with only your imagination to work on that strip of blackness between the door and the frame, you were able to conjure up more evil, more skeletons, more snakes and rats and spiders than existed in all creation. At night the path to hell began in the hallway of your apartment.

Ironically, that same closet inspired good memories. It always reminded you of another closet your parents had had. That closet had a unique feature in that it was situated over a wash basin and drain in the basement. From time to time, water bugs would find their way up to that closet and eventually into the house. You were afraid of them. But Janet, who was two back then, had no fear. She was only curious. And whenever she saw one, she would grab it with her little hand and try to put it in her mouth. At least twice, Mama caught her just as she was about to stuff one of those brown, bulbous creatures with kicking legs and flailing antennas into her gapped face. You were there both times, and your feelings about the rescue were mixed. On the one hand, you were glad your little sister was saved from eating what for all you knew could have been a poisonous morsel. On the other hand, you were disappointed because you wanted to see her face when she bit it. Maybe they tasted good!

Unlike the earlier closet, this closet slanted down under the stairs creating a space way in the back that even in the daylight looked like a void. It was always dark, always black. When Big Ma first moved you into that apartment, you always avoided even looking all the way into that closet. But when you got older, you would hide in the far reaches of that closet from Janet because you knew she was still afraid of it, and that she thus would be unable to find you there.

One day while hiding there, you noticed that the wall you used to rest your weight on wasn't really a wall. Its texture was too smooth. It gave too easily under the pressure of your thumb. It was a suitcase. You wondered why it was stuck way in the back, and not up near the front with the rest of the luggage. You gripped the handle and tried to lift it. It was full, and it was heavy.

You were in your G-man stage then. G-men always had things to help them on the job, so you had things, gadgets. You had decoder rings, pocket flash lights, dog whistles that humans couldn't hear, pocket knives with can openers, nail clippers, cork screws and screw drivers. You even had your own pepper spray which you made yourself. It consisted of a nose spray bottle that you filled with household cleaners that had warning labels on them. If the label said keep away from the eyes, you put some in. You wanted to try it on Reggie, but you were afraid to.

The suitcase in the closet was a dream come true. You pretended it was an enemy stash that you had been assigned to explore. The problem was that you couldn't let on that you knew it was there. If you let on, the owner might move it before you had a chance to explore it, discover his secret identity, and crack the case. Your plan was simple. You would fake being sick one Sunday so that Big Ma and Janet would go to church without you. Reggie was never around on Sunday mornings, or if he was, he would be hung over until afternoon.

On the appointed day, you got your G-man stuff, and slipped into the closet. In the dim yellow light from your little flashlight, you examined the case. It was big. This case was bigger than any of the other pieces of luggage in the closet. And although it had felt smooth to the touch in the dark, in fact, it was alligator skin. Using the various items in your pocket knife, you tried to pick the lock. After about fifteen minutes, you simply pushed the button. It was open.

You lifted the lid slowly, your fingers trembling. The scent from inside the case was a mixture of sweat and dust and soap and the hint of a perfume or cologne. There was a diary on top. It was black with the word 'Diary' and the year, 1947, etched in the front in gold letters. You flipped quickly through the pages just to see how many have entries. The script was flowery; the ink was peacock blue. It was about a quarter full. You took it out and put it on the floor by your ankle.

Most of the items were women's clothing. Panties, bras, four cotton blouses, two wool sweaters, a couple of pairs of gabardine pants, a couple of skirts, stockings, socks, slip-on high-heels. Then there were two pairs of white men's socks and another diary. It had the same black and gold lettered outside, but the handwriting inside was rapidly scrawled block lettering. Mostly done in black ink and pencil, it too was about a quarter full. You put it with the other one on the floor.

You ran your hand along the inside perimeter checking for secret compartments. It was solid. You checked the lid and for a false bottom. Nothing. You rubbed all along the outside surface just in case you missed something the first time around. It was clean. You put the clothes back in and closed it up. Then it hit you. The message was in the diaries. You remembered that you didn't bring your decoder ring. That's ok. You would get it later.

You reckoned the diary in black ink and pencil was your father's. His entries were short and crisp and infrequent. Most of the entries were poems. He used the diary as a notebook.

3 Jan '47

Sadie is already starting to get on my nerves about this trip. Hey, man, all I want to do is write my poems, not some travel log.

4 Jan '47

Said goodbye to Hattie and Mildred tonight. Sure can't let Sadie see this one.

7 Jan '47

The old girl looked nice this evening, or maybe it was the sunset. She inspired me to write a new piece. I'm going to rock her good tonight.

8 Jan '47

What is it with women and sex after they get married? I put my best shit on that woman, and she hardly wanted to come. She couldn't hold it, though. As she came, I put my finger on her button. She bucked like a pony for five solid minutes! Then she acted like I shouldn't have done it. You don't give it to them, they complain; you give it to them good, they complain. What the hell's going on?

31 Jan. '47.

She caught me. Just as I was about to come. Damn! Why couldn't she have waited another two minutes? She made me swear to stop seeing her. Naturally, I swore. I had my legs crossed.

The one with the peacock blue ink must have been your mother's.

Thursday, January 2, 1947.

Dear Diary, I am so excited. Bill and I are scheduled to leave in four days for Paris. I can scarcely wait. Maybe I'll run into Josephine Baker. If we both take lots of notes as we agreed to do, we should have more than enough material for a book.

Saturday, January 4, 1947.

Dear Diary, we had a long talk with Ashanti and Janet, and they— at least he— understand that they will be staying with Aunt Verlene until we get back.

Started gathering up stuff to pack.

Sunday, January 5, 1947.

Finished packing today. I just know I won't be able to sleep. Last night, he was strangely preoccupied, so he didn't even ask. He knows I don't want any more children. Why doesn't he just stop wanting it? We are intellectual beings, spiritual beings. Why must he always be an animal? Why can't he love me for my mind?

Monday, January 6, 1947.

On the train at last! We'll be in New York tomorrow, and on the boat tomorrow night. I'm going to miss the kids, but Bill and I need to do this. This might be our last hope. Janet screamed hysterically as we got on. Little man fought hard to hold his back, as did I. Bill was stoic.

Tuesday, January 7, 1947.

This ship is huge! It's not like the cargo ships we traveled to and from Liberia on. This thing has decks and games and chairs and white people calling me madam in this cute little French accent.

I had forgotten how boats rock back and forth, to and fro on the waves. I hope I don't get sick like I did on our last trip. This is a big ship. Maybe I won't. So far, it hasn't rocked a lot because the weather is good.

We watched the sunset together, orange and gold and pink on clouds that looked like mountains on the horizon. He put his arm around me.

Wednesday, January 8, 1947.

I married a pervert!

Thursday, January 9, 1947.

I hate him! Why can't we just do normal sex like everybody else? The missionary position! That's it! I'm through! No more sex! Beginning today, our marriage is going to be spiritual, intellectual.

Friday, January 31, 1947.

I caught them in the bed! Bill and this little girl from the ship. She looked about fourteen. Bill swore she was eighteen. Like that mattered! And he tried to blame it on me! ME! All I ever did was love him and have his babies. How could he do this to me?! I am so humiliated. I made him swear to never ever do it again.

There are lots of entries about shopping and outdoor cafes and great museums. Then there is the final entry.

Saturday, March 1, 1947.

Things seem to be back to normal, but they're not. Bill is writing some good stuff. So am I. I love this town. The sights, the clubs, the people are all wonderful. I wish America could be more like this. But Bill cannot leave these young French girls alone. I hate them.

We're going to the mountains. I am going to confront him, and settle this once and for all.

V

Phyllis blinks at you. "'Shanti," he says with a tone of surprise in his voice, "fancy seeing you at my front door."

"I've been driving around all day. I need a place to stay for a little while." You wish you didn't feel so glad to see him. You tell yourself it's merely because this is a safe haven, but you can feel your dick getting thick.

"Come on in." He stands aside and opens the door wide. "Are you hungry? I don't have any lamb stew left, but I'm sure I can find something." He is wearing loose jeans and a baggy grey sweatshirt. He is barefoot, and his toenails are pink having had the red lacquer removed. He gives a whole new meaning to being barefoot in the kitchen.

"I can pay you," you say. You want to keep it strictly business.

"I'm not a prostitute. I will give it to you for free."

"That's not what I'm talking about, and that's not why I'm here."

"But you are here none the less." He bats his eyes at you. "And so soon at that. What has it been? Three days?"

He leads you to the kitchen. You sit in the same chair as before.

"The police are after me for a murder I didn't commit."

"That's what they all say."

"But this time it's true."

"They all say that, too."

Phyllis bends over to check the lower shelves of the refrigerator. After a moment, he says, "I can fix you an omelet." He slides his hand into his rear pocket, then takes it out and pats himself on the ass. He stands up and faces you, "Interested?"

"I'm not interested in your ass," you answer.

"I meant the omelet, silly. I already know your feelings about my ass."

"Thanks, an omelet would be nice."

He breaks three eggs in a bowl, and begins to beat them. "So who got killed?" he asks.

You tell him.

"How was he killed?"

You tell him that, too.

"Do you know who's working the case?" He puts some oil in a skillet and lights a flame under it.

"Detective Middleman," you answer.

"Arnold Middleman?"

"Yeah, Arnie," you say. "Do you know him?"

"I know *of* him."

"How?"

"I work at the police station in your district." He pours the eggs into the skillet.

"Doing what?" You can hear the surprise in your own voice.

"I'm a clerk for one of the judges over there." He sprinkles some grated cheese into the skillet. He turns the omelet once, then twice, then folds it and slides it onto a waiting plate. After placing it before you, he fetches some silverware, and toasts some dark brown bread. He butters it and walks around next to you. He accidentally-on-purpose brushes his hip against your shoulder, and places the toast on your plate next to the eggs. You imagine you can smell the oil he uses, and the thickness in your pants grows. Maybe you're *not* imagining it. He moves back around the table and sits down.

"So what do you know about this Middleman?" you ask. You stuff a forkful of eggs into your mouth, and bite a corner of toast. You can feel yourself forcing your eyes to focus on your plate. You don't want him to see you staring at him.

"Not a lot," he answers, "but he has a reputation for being thorough."

"Meaning?"

"Meaning if he arrests you, you'll probably be convicted. He's lost a few, but not many"

"Thanks a lot," you say. Suddenly, the eggs don't taste as good as they did. You didn't like the little creep to begin with, and you like him even less now.

"Wait a minute," he says standing up abruptly. "There was an article about him in the Times not long ago which I saved. I'll get it." He leaves the room.

By the time he returns, you are finished eating. It is immediately clear what took him so long. The jeans and sweatshirt are gone. He's wearing a loose-fitting, mid-thigh length yellow dress with short bloused sleeves. He walks right over next to you and, lifting the skirt up just high enough for you to see that he isn't wearing any underwear, sits his bare behind on the table. He crosses his legs, and arranges the skirt neatly over his thighs. He gives you the article. You can smell that he has just taken a shower. It is all you can do to contain your excitement, but you don't want him to know. In fact, you wish it were not true that you even feel excitement. In fact, it pisses you off. Men don't fuck other men, at least not by choice. And you catch yourself wondering if these were the kind of thoughts Reggie had. Was he conflicted in the same way? Is it possible that he had more trouble fucking you than you had getting fucked? For you, the issue was simple. You were doing it to protect you sister. You had no choice. But he did. He controlled everything.

The article is short, and it's not about Middleman at all. It's about an increase in the number of claims of police brutality against the police department in recent months. Middleman is merely quoted a couple of times defending the department's record.

"Interesting," you say.

Phyllis takes the article from you and puts it on the table, then places your hand on his knee. "How so?" he asks.

You rub his knee gently, then you rub his thigh like you would rub a woman's. Now *you* have the choice. You don't have to do this. His leg feels like a woman's, soft and smooth, not hard and hairy like a man's. "Maybe surprising is a better word. It's surprising that you would have saved this article."

"It's not all that surprising," he says. "The big bazooka used to live here until last week."

You pull your hand away. "I thought you said you knew *of* him."

"That too," he says, putting your hand back on his knee. "In fact, his gun is still here, upstairs in a little safe he bought. He thinks I don't know the combination."

"I need to be somewhere where he can't find me," you say pulling your hand away again.

"And this is it," he says putting your hand onto his knee again.

"This is *not* it," you say. You stand up and walk to the other side of the kitchen. "One call from you and I'm toast."

"Why would I make that call?"

"I don't know, maybe to get back in good with the big bazooka."

"I'm the one who ended it."

"Ok," you say, "then he might come stalking around here trying to get his woman back."

"In that relationship, *he* was the woman. And he knows better than to come sneaking around here like some love struck schoolgirl." For just a moment reflecting on his relationship with Middleman, he slips out of character. His voice is a man's again. Then he slips back in. "*I* wanted to be the woman, so I broke it off, and I found you." He bats his eyes at you. His lashes are long and dark. Certainly longer than Jean's and maybe longer than Alice's.

Looking away, you tell him, "There is no 'Shanti and Phyllis.'"

"But you're here, and that's what counts."

"Listen," you tell him, "I am using you. They came to arrest me today, and I had to get out of my apartment fast. I'm here because this is the only place I know that I can go that nobody I know knows about. So let's not fool ourselves. I hate that I have to trust you, but I don't see that I have a choice. My only hope is that you like my dick enough to not call Middleman until I have figured out what I should do next." Shit! You hadn't meant to offer up your dick. Was that some kind of Freudian slip? Poking a hole in the scrim for this ridiculous act?

"Sex for room and board?" he asks.

"You got it. There is no love here, and like I said before, I don't do mama." What? Was denying love and not doing mama supposed to clean up for wanting to stick your dick in his ass? You sounded like Reggie calling you the faggot in order to cover up his own lust for a young boy.

"Ok," he says, "but I want it on demand. I will do all the shopping and cooking so you won't have to go out unless you want to."

"Like any other woman."

"Like any other woman. Do we have a deal?"

It worked. He doesn't know that you can't wait to poke him. He thinks you're cutting a business deal. Now if you could just convince yourself.

"Do we have a deal?" he asks again.

"Yes," you answer, "we have a deal."

"Good," he says, then he swivels his behind across to a corner of the table next to you. He lies all the way back pulling his dress up around his waist. He hikes his knees as close to his chest as he can get them, and opens them as wide as he can get them. His butt is right at the edge of the table. The oil on his rectum shines in the light from the ceiling. He looks at you standing two feet away looking at his bottom. "What are you waiting for?" he asks. "It's time to consummate the contract."

He looks so small lying there, so fragile. This time, it wasn't your imagination. You did smell the oil. You unzip your pants and let them drop to the floor. You fondle yourself in order to cover up the fact that your dick was already hard. Then you move to the corner of the table and rub the head of your dick across his rectum a couple of times. His breath quickens. So does yours, but you conceal it. You play it off. Finally, rising up on your tiptoes for better leverage, you push it in as far as it will go.

He grips the edge of the table to keep himself from sliding away. You begin rocking inside him to a slow cadence and he rocks his butt up and down to match you. To support your weight as you cantilever forward, you rest your palms on the edge of the table next to his hands. Feeling the closeness, he moves his grip from the table to your wrists, caressing them at first, then gripping them with surprising strength.

You remember the picture in his bedroom of him staring up at his mother who is looking sternly at the camera. He has that same look in his eyes now looking up at you.

You pull and push into him non-stop. You feel your body begin to glow with sweat. His face and neck and shoulders are becoming moist as well.

"Are you near coming, yet?" you ask.

"I'm trying to make *you* come," he says.

"This isn't for *me*," you counter, "it's for you."

You stop and stand up. He loosens the grip on you wrists. You slid you dick out slowly, and Phyllis sits up on the side of the table. You pull out a chair and sit down. Your dick is soft by now. Phyllis scoots off the table and moves to the sink where he wets a piece of paper towel and begins cleaning his ass.

"I won't always come," you say.

"You were holding back."

"So what if I was?"

"Yeah," he says, "so what if you were?" He throws the paper towel into the garbage, and sits in a chair across from you. He tilts his pelvis a little to one side to keep his weight off his rectum.

"So now what?" you ask, your pants still around you ankles. Before he can answer, you remember that you haven't talked to Jean since leaving the building this morning. "I need to make a phone call," you say.

"Don't call anyone you know from here on the land line," he says, "they might have caller ID and be able to trace you here."

"Good point," you say, "I'll call from a public phone." You reach for your pants.

He passes you his cell phone. "Just use this."

VI

One of the most vivid memories you have of the new west side neighborhood is of seeing two men, white men, both in their early twenties, walking along 16th Street. They had the sculptured bodies of super heroes. You were into comic books at the time-- Superman, Batman, Captain Marvel-- and you always wanted muscles like they had. With muscles like those, you could protect yourself and Janet from Reggie. But you were a skinny kid. You had never as much as seen anyone in real life with muscles like those. Then, in the middle of January, with the temperature hovering right around zero, here they came. They wore jeans and work shirts unbuttoned to the navel. You supposed their shirts were unbuttoned because shirts were not made that were big enough to fit those massive pectorals. The sleeves were short and wrapped tight around huge biceps. You wanted to ask them how they got those beautiful builds. But you dared not. And you didn't know any other white people well enough to ask instead. You imagined that they were costumed crime fighters trying in vain to walk incognito among us. You wondered what colors their capes were. And You didn't believe her when Big Ma said they were merely a couple of showoffs trying to catch colds, walking around dressed like that in this weather. It was cold enough that exhaled breath hung in the air like a miniature cloud. You kept their secret, though. You never told her that men like that didn't catch colds.

One Saturday a month later, your sister, Janet, and you were out playing in the snow. It snowed a lot back then. And Janet and you would throw snowballs with Raymond, the landlady's son. He was Janet's age, but as big as you. Because of his size, you always thought he could play hard like the big kids. He couldn't. He was a crybaby.

He and Janet together in a snow fort were no match against you. You learned years later that he died trying to get into the paratroopers. His chute didn't open. He was an only child, and his mother grieved for years. You remember wondering if he had over extended himself trying to live down a childhood reputation. When you were kids, he couldn't stand snow in his face. You *wanted* snow in your face! But he never obliged because he knew you would reciprocate. You needed some competition.

That's when you saw him. You called him Jake, but you never learned his name. He and two other white boys were throwing snowballs down the block in front of his house. He was smaller than they were, but he was feisty and he had a good aim. They were no competition for him. To your child's mind, he seemed like the perfect foil. You wanted to take him on.

His was the last white family on the block. The other two boys lived two or three blocks away. You realize now that his father had probably told him not to play with colored kids. "Colored" hadn't become "black" or "African-American" yet. But you were stunned when you ran down to get into their game, and they all ran away.

You told Big Ma what had happened, and, with a nervousness in her eyes that expressed a mixture of shame and fear and hatred and disgust, she told you the facts of life. Naturally, you made no further attempt to make contact. In fact, you didn't see him again until the spring.

The first time he saw you, he spat on the ground, then turned and ran. The next time, he threw rocks. His aim wasn't as good with rocks as with snowballs, but he was annoying. Big Ma told you to come in the house whenever he threw at you or your sister. That only made things worse. When he discovered he could run you in the house at will, you were at his mercy. It wasn't long before you decided to stop running.

Jake had an older brother, Al, who was about fifteen years old. Because of his age, you knew less about Al than you knew about Jake. Your only impression of him is one of speed-- whizzing by at top speed chasing or being chased by some other older kid at school, or cruising by on his bicycle leaning at a precarious angle, hair blowing in the wind. The rumor was that he wasn't very bright, and that he had been kept back a semester in school. You can remember folks rolling their eyes in a way that they wouldn't when discussing the mental skills of one of your friends or their siblings. It was understandable that a black person was having trouble learning. But for a white boy to be doing poorly in school meant that he was especially slow. "Ain't nothin' like a dumb white boy."

News of what went on in the upper grades rarely filtered down to the fifth and sixth grades. But this particular week, it did. Al had been suspended-- again. For fighting-- again. But for some reason, it was especially serious this time. The father was up at school; the mother was crying. Rumor had it that Al was being kicked out for good. Jake was there crying with his mother. Out of earshot, some of the older black kids were saying that being kicked out wasn't that big a deal for a white boy. After all, he was white. He would get by.

Al apparently didn't know that. The following Saturday, you saw him riding his bicycle in the direction of school. He rode with, you thought, an uncustomary heaviness. His pedal strokes were slow and measured. It was spring, and Fat Boy, a new kid your age who had just moved in down the street, and you were playing strike out. He always pitched; you always caught. Roy Campanella was your hero. Fat Boy wanted to be the first black pitcher in the majors. You saw Al ride by behind Fat Boy, who was winding up preparatory to delivering his fast ball. About an hour later, Al streaked by again. You almost missed him because you were basking in the cheers the crowd heaped on you for having just thrown out at second the fastest man in baseball. Al was pumping as hard and fast as he could. You remember wondering what his hurry was.

Fifteen minutes later, you heard the fire trucks. It took about five minutes to douse the flames. In fact, the fire was out and the trucks were gone before you even knew for sure that there was a fire nearby, that the fire was at the school, in the office, started by some skinny kid on a bicycle.

Fat Boy and you ran around to see. By now, the neighborhood was humming with rumors about massive damage to the school. You couldn't believe your luck, and you wanted to confirm the rumors before Monday rolled around and you got up for nothing.

Approaching the building from a block away, it was not obvious that there had even been a fire. You inspected the front, then walked along the south wall. Nothing. Three-quarters of the way along the back of the building, you saw wet paper lying about on the ground. It seemed too little to be evidence of the massive damage you were hoping for, but it was evidence that maybe there was more to be found. You examined the entire back wall. No charred bricks; no sagging walls. There was one broken window, the window through which this paltry find had been flung. You walked the rest of the way around the building. Nothing.

To say you were disappointed was an understatement. You were crushed. On the way over, you had made plans for Monday. You were going to get up only a little later than you would have had you gone to school. You were going to work on Fat Boy's fast ball. Then you were going to work on your swings. At lunch you were going to write letters to the Sox and the Cubs to find out about tryouts. Within ten days, you were going to be the only non-adults in all of baseball. And with the money you earned, you were going to buy cars for your mothers. Not Cadillacs, because you wanted to spend the money wisely. You would buy Pontiacs that were weighted low in the back with the spare tires on the back bumper and rear fender skirts and mud flaps studded with red and yellow jewels. You would have two aerials in the back with fox tails. You would take the hood ornament off, fill in the holes and paint it over with the same color as the car, candy apple red.

Then you would buy houses. Yours was going to be big enough for Big Ma and your sister everybody in the family. All the members of both your families were going to be set for life. Except for one thing. The school didn't burn down. Alas, when Monday rolled around, you would have to study arithmetic and penmanship. Spend the day making circles that stayed between the lines, and ovals that tilted slightly to the right. Dividing numbers that almost never seemed to come out even anymore. What a waste. You could have lived extraordinary lives. Now you would be relegated to the mundane and pedestrian.

With downcast eyes, you began the long walk back. Fat Boy kicked a piece of the debris from the fire. And for the first time since you had gotten there, you saw what it was. It was paper. Apparently, Al had started the fire in the supply cabinet figuring that all that paper was the perfect place to torch the school. Very little of it, however, actually burned, and the firemen threw reams of barely singed paper out the window. Now, there it lay-- some of it wet, most of it not-- in odd shapes and sizes in random piles on the ground.

"Wow," you said, "look at all this paper."

"Damn," Fat Boy said, "this is like a gold mine."

You gathered as much as you could carry that was salvageable.

"They just threw this stuff away!" Fat Boy said.

You looked at all of this paper weighing heavy in your arms, more paper than you had ever seen outside the store. "I'm gon' write a book," you said.

"I'm gon' write *two* books."

You stashed your treasure in a tool cabinet built under the stairs that led from your back porch to the upstairs back porch, because Big Ma wouldn't let you store it in the house. You hadn't noticed before then, but the stack reeked of smoke. You didn't care. Sitting under those stairs staring at those stacks of paper was mesmerizing. You began to imagine yourself writing things, long things that required lots of thought. You wanted to write stuff with big words. You didn't know what it would be. But you knew it would be important. You lapsed into a trance staring at that paper. You couldn't wait until Monday rolled around so you could take some of your new-found treasure to school.

You never saw Al again after that day. The rumor was that he had been sent to reform school.

There was a vacant lot around the corner from your house that you liked to play in. Jake liked to play in it, too. It had lots of tall grass and sticks and old tires to play jungle and army just like the house on 35th Street. You were playing, and after about thirty minutes, Jake came up and decided that he wanted to use the lot. He threw a couple of rocks at you. Since he was between you and the house, there was no conscious decision to be made. You ducked once. You ducked again. While you were down, you picked up a nice jagged piece of sidewalk, about three inches across. Peering through the grass, you waited until he dropped down in search of more stones. While he was down, you threw your rock. He raised up right in its path. It struck him dead center on the forehead. He grabbed his face and dropped to the ground. You thought he might be looking for more rocks, so you scrambled around for some, too. He raised up mad and crying. The game was over. "Now look what you did," he said. Blood was streaming down his face. He took off down the alley for home.

You only saw him once again after that day. He never came out. You were hoping he would, so you could tell him you were sorry. And you were. You meant to hit him, but you didn't mean to hurt him. The last time you saw him, he and his mother and father, a big man with brown hair and blue overalls, came down their front steps and climbed into their Chevy Belair. His father stopped for a long pause staring at you standing in front of your house. He knew you were the one who had hurt his boy. A glance from the boy told you that he had not told his father about all those times he had thrown rocks at you. You could tell that he, too, was sorry for the way things had turned out.

Two weeks later, they moved. Your feelings were mixed. You felt sorry for Al. Being dumb was no reason to have to wind up in a reform school. As for Jake, you would no longer have to worry about him throwing rocks at you. But also the last person who could tell you how to get those muscles was gone.

VII

The phone rings. Jean answers it. "Baby girl," you say.

"'Shanti," she says. "Where are you? I've been so worried!"

"You said get out, and I did."

"Good thing, too. The place has been crawling with cops and reporters."

"What do the reporters want?"

"Apparently, violence in a Sheridan Road highrise is a big deal."

"These folks need a life," you say. "What about the cops? Are they still around?"

"No," she answers, "they're gone. But the building office has some of that yellow barrier tape at the door."

"Ok," you say, "I need a favor. I didn't have time to pack, so I need for you to use your key to my apartment, and get some of my clothes and things, and bring them to your apartment. I'd feel a lot more comfortable sneaking to your place than to mine."

"When will you be here?"

"Probably not before tomorrow evening, but get the stuff tonight just in case."

"Where are you staying," she asks.

"With a friend," you answer. "But I don't want you to have any numbers where to reach me just yet."

"Are you staying with another woman?"

"No, it's a man."

"Oh," she says sounding relieved. "That's ok." Then she says, "I love you."

"I love you, too, honey," you say, "and I'll try to see you soon."

Poor Jean. She so fears that you will leave her. What happened to the soldier who saved you those many years ago? For that matter, where is the soldier who saved you yesterday? She can be so confident, so strong. What changes a person that way? What changes a person at all? Look at you. Yesterday, everything was fine. Today, with almost no warning, you're on the run from the law. This is like life imitating art. You've heard it a million times. One minute it was this way, the next minute it was that. But you're never ready for it. And the irony is that it never seems likely that the next minute from now-- whenever now is-- will produce a change. Why is that? Why does it always seem that life is a smooth, homogenized continuum, and that sudden change is an anomaly?

"Life is both," Phyllis answers, "a smooth, homogenized continuum of sudden change. What you see is what you decide to see."

"That's ridiculous," you counter. "life is supposed to be straight like an arrow."

"It is straight, that is until it changes."

"And it's not supposed to change."

"But it *does* change," Phyllis says.

"But it's not *supposed* to."

"But it is what it is."

"Yes," you say, "but that's not the way it is supposed to be."

"But that's the point I'm trying to make. It *is* supposed to be that way. All death is sudden change! Look around. People die all the time. Young people die all the time. Big wigs get assassinated. King, the Kennedys, John Lennon, Malcolm X, Gandhi, Marilyn Monroe. The list goes on forever. All cut down too soon, changing the continuum."

"But they're not supposed to."

"What? Are people not supposed to die?"

"Yes," you answer, "just not like that."

"I have fallen in love with an idiot!"

"What do you mean 'fallen in love?'"

"See," he says, "it just happened."

"What happened?"

"It changed."

"*What* changed?"

"The continuum just changed."

"Huh?"

"The continuum . . . just . . . changed."

"I heard what you said, but I didn't see the change."

"Sometimes, we miss life's changes. But when I said I had fallen in love with you, everything changed. Your ignorance *vis-a-vis* us got killed."

"Nothing changed, because I don't love you."

"You'll see," he says, "our fucks won't be quite as chilli as the one we just had."

He yawns and stretches and announces that he is going to bed. "You coming, too?" he asks.

"Shortly," you say.

"Don't keep me waiting," he says. "A deal is a deal."

You check the fridge for something to drink. He has cans of mineral water, so you drink one. You find the bathroom, and you take a piss and a shower. You're trying to let some time pass because you don't want him to think you are anxious. But you are. Why? Fucking some dude in the ass don't make you a faggot. It makes *him* one. But suppose you love him while you're doing it? Just suppose. But you don't. So what's the problem? You crawl into bed.

Phyllis is lying on his back staring at the ceiling. "The nature of life is like the nature of God," he says. "It has many facets and many layers."

"God is love," you answer.

"God is hate," he answers back.

"And you think I'm the one who is the idiot here?"

Phyllis pauses a moment. "Does Jesus sit at the right hand of God?"

"Absolutely!"

"Who sits at the left hand of God?"

You hesitate trying to recollect your Sunday school teachings. Where is Applecrusher when you need her. Finally you answer, "Nobody."

"Wrong."

"The Holy Spirit."

"Wrong."

"Then who?" you ask.

"Satan."

"*Satan?!*"

"Satan."

"Now I *know* you're an idiot. Satan is a fallen angel. He tried to challenge God. How can he sit by God?"

"He's not fallen," Phyllis says, "he just has a bad reputation because he's the one who gets to do the dirty work."

"We are going to be struck by lightning before sunrise." You turn your back to him and cradle your pillow. It's amazing how smart people can be so misguided.

"Don't go to sleep yet," he says, "I'm not through."

"Well I am," you answer.

"Don't be so thin skinned.'"

"Don't be such an ass."

"I though you liked my ass."

"You know what I mean."

He pauses a moment, then says, "Don't be so afraid of the truth."

"I'm not afraid of the truth."

"Then why can't we talk about God?"

"Because you don't know what you're talking about."

"You're afraid to hear the truth."

"The truth," you say, "is that God is real, God is alive, and God is good."

"The truth," Phyllis says, "is that neither the existence nor non-existence of God can be proven or disproven. And the same holds true for any kind of value judgment about Him."

"What?!"

"Language and rational thought are not adequate to deal with metaphysical concepts."

"Just tell me this, do you believe in God?"

"I *know* there is a God."

"Are you a Satan worshiper?"

"Of course not."

"Then why are you talking like one?"

"I'm not."

"You are."

"I'm not."

"Then what are you talking about?"

"The nature of the reality, seen and unseen."

"Ok," you say. "What is the nature of reality, seen and unseen?" You really want to drop this stupid discussion, but he seems bent on expressing his views. What is it about people that they always want to convert you to their point of view?

He sits up in the bed, and rests his back against the bookcase he uses as a headboard. He'd better be careful lest his mother's eyes burn little pin holes in his skin. "All the major religions have it wrong," he says. "Or if they have it right, the true nature of God is obscured from the flock. Even the highest leaders probably don't know what the prophet really meant in his writings. Couple that with the political agenda these leaders have, and it is a wonder that anything worthwhile gets to the flock at all."

"You're losing me." You don't have the heart to tell him you are only half listening.

"I guess I'm losing myself."

"Then keep it simple."

"Ok," he says, "consider this. Could Pinocchio challenge Geppetto?"

"No," you answer, "Pinocchio is a puppet. He does nothing until Geppetto pulls his strings."

"Correct," he says. "Now consider that Satan exists only because God continues to allow him to exist. Satan did not and could not create himself, and he cannot continue to exist of his own volition." He pauses, then asks, "Can Satan challenge God?"

"Satan has free will," you answer, "and he can use that free will to challenge God."

"Wrong! He can use that free will to sass God, to hurl insults, to talk shit. But God's power cannot be challenged. God *is* power! There is no power aside from God. Therefore, any power Satan has, he got from God."

"What's your point?"

"My point is that Satan works for God."

"You're insane!"

"The universe," he continues, "is like arithmetic. There are positive numbers and there are negative numbers. Zero is in the middle, neither positive nor negative. The positive numbers are love, joy, bliss. The negative numbers are hate, fear, guilt. Jesus presides over the positive numbers. Satan presides over the negative ones. God is the zero and all the positive and negative numbers combined. He is centered between the two extremes in a void of indifference." He pauses a moment, then says, "Then there's us. Just as God runs from positive infinity through zero to negative infinity, we each run from positive one through zero to negative one. We are created in God's image, and God doesn't care what we do."

"Unless we sin . . ."

"There is no sin."

". . . and get sent to hell."

"There is no hell."

"So everybody goes to heaven?"

"There is no heaven."

"Was there a Christ?"

"Have you been listening? Of course there was– *is* a Christ."

"Then what did he do?" you ask.

"He made a bid to rid the world of the debilitating and crippling hatred, fear and guilt that keeps men stunted. The earth was overrun with negative numbers. So he threw in some positive numbers to balance things out."

"What about original sin?"

"Forget about sin!"

"But sin is real," you say.

"Sin is a philosophical construct designed to keep people in line."

"Me being in this bed with you is a sin."

"Then why are you here?"

"I have no place else to go."

"Why were you here three nights ago?"

"It seemed like an ok thing to do at the time."

"Are you going to burn in hell for it?"

"No."

"And why not?"

"Because I'm saved."

"Meaning?"

"My sins are forgiven."

"Meaning?"

"Meaning I have no sin."

"Fine!" he said, "but now I ask you what is the difference between having no sin and sin not existing?"

"For me," you say, "none. But to the unsaved, a lot."

"The unsaved being those who have not taken Jesus Christ as their personal savior?"

"Exactly."

"What about those people who have never heard of Jesus Christ?"

"That's a problem."

"And the solution?"

"They burn in hell, I suppose."

"You mean they will burn in hell because God chose not to allow them to bump into the notion of Jesus Christ?" He snorts, "That hardly seems fair."

"How come you know so much about this shit?" you ask.

"I was going to become a priest."

"So what happened?"

"One of them fucked me, and I decided that I liked it."

"You could have still become a priest."

"You're right," he says. "The world is full of faggot priests. But I couldn't be one of them. It's like I said before, it is not easy being honest."

You ponder for a moment the lateness of the hour. "So what is the solution?" you ask.

"Simple," he says. "When Jesus said that you cannot get to the Father except through Him, He didn't mean Him *qua* Jesus, the man. He meant Him *qua* Spirit. And every act of faith invokes Him *qua* Spirit whether or not the actor knows or has even heard of Him *qua* Jesus, the man."

"But the man Himself was special," you say.

"Yes, but only because of the spirit that dwelt within." He pauses for a moment, then says, "Picture it like this. God is the water in a pond. The surface of the pond is concealed in a thick cloud which means the water cannot be seen. Around the pond, there is a sandy beach. Along the beach, there are diving boards at different heights extending out over the water. There are piers and wharfs built out into the water. All of these structures represent different religions or belief systems. And all of them have one flaw."

"Namely?"

"If you walk to the end of the board or pier or wharf and look down, you can't see the water. The only way to get to the water is to jump into the cloud. Even if you walk towards the water from the beach itself, you cannot get to the water without becoming engulfed in the cloud first."

"So Christ is the cloud."

"Exactly!" Phyllis says. "Christ is the cloud! The problem is that priests and preachers and imams and gurus would have you believe that the only way to God is whichever board or pier or wharf they happen to be standing on at the moment. And except for the 'only' part, they're right! All these structures will get you to the water. But none of them can bypass the cloud. The only way to the water is to make the existential leap of faith into the cloud."

You catch yourself jerking involuntarily, and you realize that you have been hearing Phyllis' words through the fog of sleep.

"Don't go to sleep yet," he says. "I want to suck your dick."

Only half awake, you turn onto your back and open your legs. He crawls between them. He cups your dick in both hands and begins to stroke it slowly up and down. He must have put oil on his hands because there is surprisingly little friction. Your dick rises to its full length, and, still stroking, he puts the head into his mouth. He matches the bobbing of his head to the strokes of his hands. Within two minutes, you can feel yourself beginning to come. Damn, he gives good head! You plant you feet and raise your hips up off the bed. Your dick is as deep in his mouth as it will go. You come, and he sucks the semen straight down. You sink back down to the bed and your whole body relaxes into a euphoric state. You can feel Phyllis groping around your testicles as you nod off to sleep.

VIII

Big Ma had to work. Reggie had a job, too. So when the summer rolled around and kids danced in the spray of the fire hydrant on the corner, raced orange-crate scooters and rode their bikes to the field house and lagoon, your sister Janet and you sat inside reading World Book Encyclopedia.

Rather, *you* read World Book. *She* read *How to Tell Your Child*. Why was it that girls always seemed to know more than boys? You were twelve; she was eight. But she knew the answers to all the unasked questions springing unbounded in your mind. It was three years before you found out that book contained a detailed description of sex and childbirth. While she read about sperm cells, you read about dinosaurs. While she looked at pictures of pregnant women, you looked at pictures of ships with tall sails. While she dreamed about feeling the kicking, you dreamed about building your boat.

Boats were the craze that summer, boats carved from cast off two-by-fours. All the boys on the block made one. Percy, Marshall, Anthony, Lamont. Sugar Baby and Fat Boy had moved by then. Each boat was fashioned after each boy's own personality.

Percy's was painted bright yellow, the same color he eventually choose for his first car. It had huge white sails that caught the wind like pockets. He bragged that his boat was the slickest and fastest one on the block.

Everybody called Percy ol' black Percy behind his back or when they were signifying on him. Most of you boys didn't signify with Percy, though. He had a quick mind and a repertoire of rhymes that made him a formidable opponent.

Percy liked to think of himself as a pretty-boy. Always talked about pussy and the girls he'd fucked. More often, he talked about the girls he wouldn't fuck, and you never saw him with a girlfriend. But he was thirteen, and to you, being thirteen was like being magic. In your heart, you couldn't wait to be thirteen, because by then, you would be able to tell similar stories.

Marshall's boat was big and crude and devoid of details. The bow was sawed at a blunt angle, and the rough surface of the wood, complete with splinters and jagged edges, was left unfinished and naked. The boys called Marshall aircraft carrier because he had a head as big as one. It was flat on top, and it even sloped in back and came to a point. Nobody ever called him that to his face, though, because Marshall was slow. He couldn't signify, and he knew it. So if you called him out of his name or talked about his mother, he would simply punch you out.

Marshall was older than even Percy, fourteen. But he got put back in school, so he ran with a younger group.

Lamont and Anthony made their boat together. They were twins. Their boat was simple, even elegant. Lamont built it; Anthony decorated it. The finished product was long and sleek with short masts and wide sails. The idea, they explained, was to minimize the drag and maximize the pull. It was painted silver and the sails were blue.

You wanted your boat to be special. Whenever you were sent to the store, you would cut through alleys and vacant lots that were way out of the way looking for pieces of wood. Not too old, not too dirty, not too much paint. Not rotted. You knew the alley behind your house. Every can, every fence, every garage, every angle in the four to six inch wide crack that ran down the center of the concrete pavement. No point in checking back there. Molloy's grocery was on the corner of 15th and Central Park, only a couple blocks away. But your wanderings took you sometimes half a mile out of the way.

Whenever Janet was along, you would have to threaten her to keep her from telling Big Ma where you had been.

"I'm telling Big Ma," she would say. "We ain't got no business being way over here on Roosevelt Road."

"You tell and I'll beat your booty tomorrow when she's at work."

Then she would start to cry. "I don't want to be in no trouble," she would say.

"Shut up," you would say. "I'm the one who'll be in trouble, not you."

"I don't want you to be in no trouble, either," she would say.

So you would walk faster pulling her along behind you while carefully scanning the way for wood.

After about two weeks, you found it. It was behind Gethsemane Garden Baptist Church where carpenters were building a couple of new rooms in the basement for Sunday School classes. It was new wood, eighteen inches long. You wondered if having been baptized there had made the difference.

"What you gon' do with this ol' smelly piece of wood," Janet asked as you gave it to her to carry.

"Make a boat."

"They still ain't gon' like you."

"They're my friends."

"They don't like you 'cause you're smart."

By now, Janet was a skinny little black girl with bamboo legs and ashy knees. Her face was the color of root beer, and her hair was parted into quarters and braided.

"That's why they beat you up."

You began by sawing the bow to a keen angle. Next, you shaped the hull by planing the corners off one of the 4-by-eighteen inch sides. You carved a subtle angle to the plane sloping sternward, sculpted the final shape to the bow, and sanded the hull smooth. Three pencil-thin masts with red silk sails, red cotton thread for rigging, and three coats of clear varnish finished it off. The silk was from a slip given to Big Ma by some man who claimed he wanted to marry her, but who Big Ma said she couldn't stand. You rescued the slip from the garbage after Big Ma threw it and the card that came with it away.

The boat was stunning. Slicker than Percy's; sleeker than Anthony and Lamont's. You named it the Sea Serpent. You tested it in the bathtub for hours to make sure it was seaworthy, that it didn't lean to one side or the other. So when the day came to test them out in the lagoon, you were ready. The only problem was, you couldn't go. The other boys wanted to meet at midday on a weekday. Big Ma was working and you had to stay home.

The boys gathered on your front porch. You could see their boats through the locked screen door. They didn't know you had even made a boat. They assumed that you wouldn't since you wouldn't be able to come to the sail off.

"My boat's gon' kick ass," Percy said holding the Golden Bomb at arm's length.

"It bet' not touch mine," Marshall said.

"I *know* it ain't gon' touch mine," Lamont said.

"I made a boat, too."

Anthony and Lamont claimed to be twins, but they didn't look any more alike than mere brothers. Lamont was tall, gangly, with a protruding Adam's apple. Anthony-- he never liked being called Tony-- was more your height, and dumpy. He had that "good" hair, the kind with the soft loose curls, that black folks all envy. Lamont, on the other hand, had cuccabugs and naps like everybody else. They were both high yellow.

"What kind of boat you got?" Anthony demanded.

"Just a plain boat," you answered.

"Go get it," Percy said, turning his head to snicker at the thought that you had built a boat.

"It's right here," you said. You lifted it up to the screen for them to see. It was complete with the name branded into the stern. You made the brands yourself from hairpins, and carefully heated each one in the blue flame of the stove until it glowed red. Then you seared the letters into the wood.

After a noticeable silence among them, Marshall said, "That is a bad motherfucker."

"Too bad you can't come sail it," Percy quipped.

Of the four of them, you liked Marshall the best. He didn't seem to mind that you had gotten a double promotion and were younger than the rest of them. Sometimes you felt sorry for him for being the oldest and slowest. Maybe he felt sorry for you for being the youngest and the smartest. Maybe that was your bond.

"Marshall can take mine and sail it with his," you said.

You watched them as they walked north towards the lagoon. Marshall lumbered along carrying two boats, one in each hand. He was bent forward as if under the weight of the responsibility. Percy, Anthony and Lamont swarmed around him like gnats, alternately soaring boats over their heads like airplanes. It was hot, ninety degrees, and the sun blazed down on their heads, and you wished you could go, too.

"You can kiss that boat good-bye," Janet said.

"Marshall will protect it."

"Marshall is too dumb to protect it."

You knew she was right.

Two hours passed before you could see them rounding the corner at 15th Street heading your way. They were subdued, even morose. Marshall lagged ten paces behind.

You hadn't left the window since they left the front porch. You spent the entire time dreaming of how dazzled they would be by your boat, imagining your boat winning the race across the lagoon in record time and them coming back with a plaque crafted on the spot by the commissioner of parks who happened to be there that day looking for boys with sailboats whose pictures he could put in the paper.

They walked straight by. Percy harrumphed once, then cut his eyes in your direction. "Pussy mouth motherfucker," he said as he walked on. When he thought he was out of earshot, he said to Anthony, "Reggie told me he fucks that nigger every day." Anthony looked around at you in disgust. "And I'll bet he *likes* it."

Marshall slowed down.

"You won," he said, then he looked away.

Janet walked in just in time to see him walk by. "I told you," she said.

"Shut up!" You snapped, fighting back the tears.

You never saw the boat again. Marshall was ashamed to ever tell you what happened to it, and the others had sworn a pact of secrecy.

IX

"Where are you staying?" Jean asks.

"I can't tell you that."

"How can I find you if I need to talk to you about the case?"

Phyllis had gone when you woke up. You looked around. You listened for a moment to the noise in the house. You were alone. You looked at his mother in the picture. Rather, she looked at you from the picture, you who let her son suck your dick, you who fucked her son in the ass. Her eyes, those burning orbs that you could feel even in a picture, told you that you were the real faggot here. Her son was a victim, because she was not there to protect him from you just like she had to protect him from his father, that spineless blob who stood staring off at the guild picture frame. You turned you eyes away and got up. You cleaned yourself and got dressed. You drove over to Sheridan Road. You didn't pull into the garage, though. Rather, you parked on a nearby side street and walked to the front of the building. You approached from the opposite side of the street so that you could see who was in the lobby before actually going in. The entire front of the lobby was glass, and you could see that it was empty. You crossed Sheridan Road and pulled open the front lobby door. Putting the lobby phone to your ear and keeping your back the camera situated over the mailboxes, you found Alice's bell and rang it. She asked who it was. You gave her your name. Before you could explain that you needed to talk to her, she buzzed you in. "Jean said to expect to see you," she said. You took the stairs rather than the elevator to her floor to avoid running into anyone you knew. The door was already open when you got around to her apartment. You walked in and closed the door behind you.

"I can't tell you that either," you say.

"Well, we have a problem."

"What's up?" you ask.

"The cops are in the building looking for you," Jean says, "that's what's up."

"How did they know I was here? I just got in."

"I don't know that part," Jean says, "but they were just getting ready to knock on my door when I walked out."

"What did you tell them?" you ask.

"Nothing. I . . ."

"They can't possibly know that I'm in this apartment," you say, "not unless you told them."

"No! No," Jean says, her voice rising. "I swear."

Alice looks at her with what you thought was a questioning expression.

"What do they plan to do?" you ask. "Go door to door?"

"No," Jean answers, "but they do plan to post guards at all the exits. Somehow, they know you're in the building."

"Did you get my things?"

"I couldn't," Jean answers. "I was afraid they would be watching me too closely."

"Ok," you say, "there is still one way they are probably not guarding. Did they see you come in here?"

"No, I waited until they were off my floor. That's what took me so long after Alice called and said you had arrived."

You have Alice check the hallway. It's clear, so you have Jean go back to her place using the elevator while you and Alice take the stairs to the first floor. Before opening the door from the stairwell to the first floor hallway, you give Alice the key to the storage room right across the hall.

"Hold the storage room door open and signal me when the guards in the lobbies at both ends of the hallway are looking the other way."

She opens the stairwell door nonchalantly, and strolls across the hall. Your pulse quickens as the officer in the rear calls out, "Miss, what time do you have?" He's testing her. Cops always have watches. You allow the stairwell door to click shut.

Alice keeps her composure, "Almost three o'clock," she answers.

"Thanks," the officer says. He is right outside the stairwell door now. "Do you know Ashanti Ra?"

"Everyone in this building knows Mr. Ra," Alice answers. "Why do you ask?"

"We need to ask him some questions, and I was wondering if you had seen him around."

"Have you checked his apartment?" she asks.

"Yes," the officer answers, "but he hasn't been there in a couple of days."

"Well, I'm sorry officer," she says. "I haven't seen him."

"If you should see him, could you give us call?" His voice fades as he heads back to the rear lobby.

"Sure, officer," Alice answers. "I would be glad to." You hear her unlock the storage room door. You crack the stairwell door to see her signal. Through the smallest opening possible, you see her check the front lobby, then the rear. She jerks her head for you to come across. The rear officer must have his back turned. Just as you are about to open the door and hop across, he says, "Oh, by the way, my name is James Stone. I work with Detective Middleman." It's Jack! You knew that voice sounded familiar. Why would a detective be guarding a door?

Alice's eyes yank wide for you to stay put. You freeze. She

composes her face and pokes her head into the hallway to look back down to the rear lobby. "I have his number," she says. She smiles at him. Then she jerks her head to one side again. You snatch the door open, and leap across. She checks the hallway in both directions, then closes the storage room door. Resting her back against it, she sighs, "That was close."

You give her a peck on the lips. "You were great," you say. Then you wind your way between the storage lockers to the two small windows facing Sheridan Road. The windows let out onto the roof the garage in the basement. Alice follows you. "One last thing," you say to her, "make sure the front guard is in the lobby. If he is in the lobby, he won't be able to see me climb down from this roof."

Alice scampers back around to the door. You hear her open it, then you hear it click shut. You hear her shuffling her feet back around to the windows. "He's in the lobby," she says.

You open the window, and lift one leg to stick it out. She grabs your arm. She gives you a kiss on the lips. "I had a good time," she says.

"It was three years ago," you answer.

"I still remember."

You make your way to the edge of the roof. Looking at the driveway below you, you realize that it is a longer drop than you had thought. As a kid, you used to jump off garages, you and Sugar Baby and Fat Boy. They were the kids who moved into the apartment down the street from you after the last white boy and his family moved out. You must have been idiots! Fat Boy was your age. His sister, Sugar Baby, was three years older. *She* was the idiot! She would dare the two of you to jump. When both of you out of good sense declined, she would jump, then turn around and dare you again. "I 'D' double dog dare you to jump," she would say. Now you *had* to jump. She was a girl, and she had already jumped. How could you say no. So, you jumped. Fat Boy twisted his knee; you sprained your ankle. A month later, after you healed up, you jumped again. This time both of you survived with no injuries.

Listening to the roar of traffic on Sheridan Road, you get down on your stomach and lower your legs over the side. You slide your belly over the gutter. You vow to work the gut off this summer. You look across at the window to the storage room. Alice is still there watching you. You kiss the air in her direction. She kisses back. Then you slide your chest over until you are hanging on by just your arms. The gutter creaks, and you catch your breath. The last thing you need is for the gutter to come crashing down with you hanging onto it. You scoot your elbows over the edge. You hang on with only your fingertips and your chin. You turn your face to one side until your chin slides off the edge. Your weight pulls you down the full length of your arms. You hang on by only your fingertips. You flex your toes down hoping against hope that they will touch the ground. They don't. The edge of the gutter begins to cut into your fingers. You ease your grip until your fingers slip off the edge. You fall for what seems like an eternity.

You hit the ground. Your ankle twists. Your knees buckle, and you thunk into the concrete pavement of the driveway with your elbow. You roll forward into the garage door with your left shoulder and the crown of your head. The thump rings in your ears as you try to get up. Weaving from side to side and without putting any weight on you right ankle, you turn to face the street. Shit! That's the same ankle you sprained when Sugar Baby made you jump.

Holding your elbow, you hobble up the incline of the driveway to the sidewalk.

X

The Gethsemane Garden Baptist Church was on the corner right across the street from your house. The pastor was Clarence Higgins, Jr. The director of the children's choir was Nancy Abercrambie. The boys called her Mrs. Applecrusher behind her back. The girls never did, but they always laughed with the boys when they did it. She was in her late twenties with a round face that still had the residue of teenage acne. She wore glasses, and she had what you thought were perfect legs and feet. You had such a crush on her that you could scarcely look her in the eye. Naturally, you thought she loved you, too, even though she was already married and you were only thirteen years old.

Her husband's name was Marvin. He sang in the adult choir, and he had a wonderful baritone voice. He sang with such passion and conviction, that it was jarring to see him come home late on Friday and Saturday nights drunk and staggering.

The Abercrambies lived on the second floor of the two story, grey stone building behind the church. Reverend and Mrs. Higgins lived on the first floor, and Mr. Abercrambie was a source of embarrassment for everyone in that building. Everyone, that is, except Clarence the third.

You worked for the church on Saturday afternoons, sweeping the sidewalks and front hallway, and occasionally mopping. The arrangement you had was that you would do the few chores they assigned, and they would pay you a few dollars to be paid after Sunday services after the collection had been taken. Big Ma didn't like the idea very much, though, because she didn't trust that Reverend Higgins would pay you. In fact, Gethsemane was not Big Ma's regular church. Her regular church was over on 36th Street near State Street. But since the move over here, that church was hard to get to on a regular basis.

Gethsemane, on the other hand, was right across the street. It was easy for you and Janet to get to every Sunday. It was important that you and Janet go, because, as Big Ma put it, she already knew the Lord. On those occasions when she went to Gethsemane, she let everyone know that she disapproved of the arrangement.

Ultimately, she was proven right. The deacons paid you promptly the first two Sundays. On the third Sunday, they paid you about two-thirds of the original agreed upon wage. On the sixth Sunday, Reverend Higgins recommended that the privilege of working for Christ and the church should be payment enough for your services. That Sunday, Big Ma terminated the contract.

That was the week you met Clarence the third. On the previous Sunday, Reverend Higgins suggested that you give Mrs. Higgins a hand around the house. He recommended that Wednesday after school would be a good day. You didn't tell Big Ma, because you knew she would have a fit. Instead, you simply went over at the appointed time. Mrs. Higgins, a short, light-skinned, dumpy woman with thick ankles and old lady comforts, had you mop the kitchen floor and empty the garbage. It struck you as odd that a man who preached that cleanliness was next to godliness would have such an incredibly filthy kitchen floor. That's when Clarence the third walked in. He went to the refrigerator, took out bread and cheese and mustard and mayonnaise. He was tall and burly like his father with big hands and a full beard. His nappy hair was thinning on top, and he was funky like he hadn't bathed in a couple of weeks. He gathered the sandwich making up like you imagined a bear would gather it up, all at once. Meats, cheese, bread, condiments all gathered against his chest and held in place by a finger or a thumb. The mustard shifted, and he almost dropped it. He caught it by shifting his hip. He hobbled over to the cutting board by the sink, and let each item roll from the cluster onto the work surface. He had to catch the mayonnaise from rolling off.

"You must be the new hired help around here," he said. His voice was surprisingly high. You had expected this big guy to have a deep base voice, but instead it was this little high thing not as deep as your own.

"I guess so," you said.

"Welcome to the mad house." He reached his hand into the package and pulled out four pieces of white bread. He arranged them on the counter. "How much are they paying you?"

You were ashamed to answer.

Sensing your hesitation, he said, "Let me guess. You're working for the glory of the Lord."

You nodded your head yes.

"Ha," he said, "I knew it. He used to get me with that one, too. Only, since I was the preacher's son, there was no way out. You still have a chance, though." He slathered mayonnaise on two of the slices, then dropped the knife on the floor. He picked it up, leaving a glob of mayonnaise behind. He slathered the rest of the bread without wiping off the knife. Reaching for the cheese, he stepped into the glob of mayonnaise and squished it. His feet were bare. They looked like short versions of his hands, thick with stubby toes and heavy, uncut toenails. "Want a sandwich?" he offered.

"No." Your answer sounded like it was delivered too quickly.

"Suit yourself," he said, stuffing a scrap of ham into his mouth. His sandwiches made, he left the kitchen tracking traces of mayonnaise in his wake.

Looking around at the floor, you began to guess at what some of the spills might be. Ketchup or barbeque sauce, gravy or chocolate, mustard or egg yoke. There were crumbs in all the corners. A small piece of cornbread lay by the stove next to a sliver of porkchop bone next to the broom. As you reached for the broom, Clarence the third startled you from the doorway. "Do you play chess? Of course you don't. Stop up front when you're done. I need to show you some moves."

You swept the kitchen and mopped it and emptied the bucket. The water was black with filth. You emptied the garbage. You headed for the living room trying to make as little noise as possible. Clarence was waiting.

"Sit down," he said, gesturing to the large leather chair across the small table from where he sat in an equally large leather chair.

You sat in the chair and discovered that it wasn't nearly as comfortable as it looked. It was too big, and the seat was slippery. Looking at the row of brass brads that appeared to hold the leather to the shiny dark wood, you got as comfortable as you could.

"The first thing you have to learn is that life is not logical. I don't mean in the sense that the existence of life defies reason, which it does, but, rather, in the sense that all day-to-day occurrences happen capriciously. The Bible said it best: The race is not to the swift. This is not a lament, merely a statement of fact. It's axiomatic! Shit happens! So you've got to learn to live with it, even plan on it. It's the only reasonable thing to do.

"The second thing you have to learn is, don't let people mess with you." He looked you in the eye waiting for your reaction.

You looked away and nodded yes.

"Look at me," he said. "Don't be afraid."

"Yes, sir,"

"Don't call me sir. Call me Clarence."

"Ok, Clarence."

"Chess is war. Chess is like life in America. In chess, white always moves first."

"Why?"

"It's the rule," he said. "But moving first doesn't mean you always win."

"Does white have an advantage?"

"Whites always have an advantage, but superior play by blacks can overcome that advantage. And then there is the luck or shit-happens factor."

"What's that," you asked.

"That's when God picks the winner." He paused. "Here are the pieces," he said, "one king, one queen, two bishops, two knights, two rooks and eight pawns." He arranges the white pieces on the board. "Put your pieces in place."

You arranged your pieces to mirror his.

"The queen goes on the square of her own color," he said.

"How does God pick the winner," you asked, changing the position of your king and queen.

"That is the question of questions," he said. "Nobody knows the answer, but I can give you an example."

You sat forward in your chair in order to better hear.

"I was in the navy on a ship in Korea," he began as he sat back in his chair forgetting, for the moment, the chess instruction. His gaze was off to the corner of the room as he remembered. He ran his fingers through his beard as he spoke. "I was below decks talking with one of my white shipmates. We were standing maybe three feet apart. With no warning, a bomb dropped between us." He shifted his gaze to you. "It was a dud. That's why it didn't explode when it hit the deck above us." He moved his gaze to the corner again. "It tore a gapping hole in the ceiling above us and in the floor between us. I looked down and saw the bomb resting two decks below where we stood. Then I looked at the guy I had been talking to." He looked at you again. "His eyes were dead," he said. "Then I saw the thin red line running straight down the center of his body, and I realized that one of the fins on the bomb as it dropped between us had cut him in half." He drew an imaginary line down his own body as he spoke. "The other two fins simply grazed by me– one on each side– on their way down. I was never even touched." He paused. "That's how God picks."

"So what did you do?" you asked.

"Nothing," he answered. "There was nothing *to* do right then. God picked me as the winner that time, but I knew that he would eventually pick me as the loser. If not today, tomorrow. If not tomorrow, next month. If not next month, next year. But sooner or later we all get picked the loser." He paused. "After the battle was over, I sank into a cold sweat thinking it could have been me. Jimmy Joe was his name. He was a white boy from Alabama. He wanted to be a painter. He wanted to move to New York and paint like the great Flemish masters. All he did in his spare time was sketch. He had pads filled with pictures of the guys on board, and of parts of the ship. We nicknamed him Artie because he was such an artist. Everybody on board liked him, and he had more talent than anyone on board that I knew. After ourselves, we all wanted him to make it through so we could say we knew him after he got famous. He was the first one to die. *That's* how God picks." He sat forward in his chair returning his attention to the game. "Here is how the pieces move." He carefully explained how each piece moved. Then, with his index finger, he began drawing small circles just above the four squares at the center of the board. "In the beginning, the fight is for these squares." He advanced his king pawn two squares.

You remembered the fourth grade. You remembered Michael Sampson. Michael Sampson was the fat, white boy who always hung his head and looked depressed anytime anyone said the word 'mister.' Little bullet-head Sammie Wilson and fat lip Melvin used to chide him and say mister over and over again just to piss him off. After a while, he would try to hit one of them, but he was too slow and awkward. You often wondered what the problem was, but whenever you broached the topic, he would turn his sad eyes away and change the subject.

Finally, about half way through the school year, while on a field trip to Brookfield Zoo, you asked him, "Why does 'mister' make you sad?"

At first, he looked at you suspiciously, squinting his sad, blue eyes. After all, bullet-head Sammie and fat lip Melvin were your friends. Then he said, "You have to promise to keep it a secret."

You promised and he began his tale. He was sad because his grandfather had been killed that previous summer by a sixteen-year-old boy they had befriended earlier that summer who always called the grandfather 'mister.' The grandfather had been teaching the two boys how to hunt in the woods, and giving lessons on the safe use of a shotgun. It wasn't clear to you how it happened, but apparently the boy left the gun loaded when he shouldn't have. When confronted by the grandfather, the boy snapped that he hadn't felt like it, and grabbed at the gun. The grandfather yanked the gun back to avoid the boy's grab. The gun fell to the floor and discharged shooting the grandfather in the thigh. He bled to death in about ten minutes.

"Damn you, boy," the grandfather had said as he and Michael fought to make the tourniquet hold in the mass of blood gushing from his leg. "You are going to pay for this."

Michael ended the story by pounding his fist on his knee and swearing the kill the boy if he ever met him again.

Oddly, or maybe not so oddly, Michael was insensitive to the loss other people suffered. About two weeks after the field trip, a substitute teacher came to your classroom. You remembered he was strange from the very beginning, because he didn't merely walk in. He looked in first. There was fear in his eyes. He looked at you and the other kids in that room as if he were looking at a pit of vipers. He pulled his head back, waited two seconds, then walked in with an affected smile. Even his footsteps were cautious.

He asked you where you had left off in your geography book. You told him. He had you open to the appropriate page and begin to read aloud as he called on you one at a time. He called on Michael. Rather, he called on Mr. Sampson. Michael stood up, his sad eyes staring at the floor.

"What's the matter, Mr. Sampson?"

"Nothing," Michael had said.

"Don't you like geography?"

"I hate geography," Michael had said. "It's got nothing to do with me."

"I used to think that," the teacher said, "before I went to Korea." He looked around the room. The fear in his eyes had changed to a measure of confidence as he convinced himself that fourth graders were not dangerous. Then his eyes changed again as he mentioned Korea. They changed to sadness. The man, tall and black and strong, almost began to cry. He searched each one of our faces for some degree of pity. "Korea was hell," he said. "I lost my best friend there about two months ago.

"We were walking among some trees when we came under fire from a North Korean tank. I jumped behind a big rock. Fred jumped behind a tree stump. I saw him eyeing a rock on the other side of the clearing, and I shouted to him to stay where he was. No, man, he said. I've got to get some better cover than this. He jumped up to run, and jumped right into the path of the next tank shell. It blew him into a thousand pieces right there before my eyes. Blood, fingers, ears, eyes, hair everywhere."

The man looked sadder than Michael ever had. His eyes were red and filled with water. He began to sniff to hold back the tears. That's when Michael let him have it.

"Don't nobody care about your old stupid friend. I'm *glad* he's dead."

Instantly, self pity turned into fear. The vipers were back, and they were striking at his most sensitive parts. The teacher stood up. He bolted for the door. The sound of the class cheering as he left could only have been hissing to his ears.

Only one person in the whole class didn't cheer at this rare and obvious victory of children over an adult. Adam Baker. Adam sat in the seat immediately to your right. You hadn't known it before that day, but Adam was a lot older than the rest of you. Adam was a veteran. Adam had been in Korea. You knew he wasn't like the rest of you even though he was short, because he smelled like a man. He wore the cologne men wore. And he didn't start with the rest of you. He started in the middle of the term, only a week or so before the field trip to Brookfield Zoo. Apparently, he had just been discharged. He never played at recess.

"You shouldn't laugh at him," Adam said to you. "I've seen lots of guys like him." No one else in the class heard his words. Only you. "That man is sick. He won't be coming back."

"How do you know?" you asked.

"I've seen this before." Adam looked at you looking back at him. "I've been to Korea," he said.

"How old are you?"

"I'm nineteen," he answered.

"What are you doing here?" The amazement in your voice surprised even you.

"I don't read so good, so they put me in this class. I won't be here long, though. I need to find a job."

"What was it like," you asked.

"It was rough. A lot of guys I know didn't make it. Some of them were killed. A lot of them ended up like teacher man. It ain't no fun spending three days and nights in a foxhole dug in the middle of a grave. Smelling the shit, hearing the bodies moan. Eating cold beans from a can while sitting in your own shit. Watching guys get their head's blown off while running across a field. His body ran two more steps before it fell and shook. It ain't pretty."

"Did you ever have to kill anybody?"

"Once or twice."

"What was it like?"

"It didn't bother me, but some guys couldn't do it."

"I could do it," you said, feeling brave. "I *know* I could do it." You pause, then ask, "what was it like?"

"The first time, it was like jumping from in front of a car before you get hit. He was running at me with a bayonet. I was holding my rifle at hip level and I shot him in the chest. He took one more step, then dropped at my feet."

"What would you have done if you had missed?"

"They teach you to fall on your back and kick the rifle barrel away with your feet," he said. "But that doesn't always work. I saw one soldier get his dick and nuts cut off trying to kick a bayonet away."

"What did the man you shot look like?"

"I don't know. As soon as I knew I was still alive, I ran for cover. I shot at a few people from behind a rock, but I don't think I hit them."

Your collective victory over teacher man seemed hollow now. Cheering that first seemed gleeful now seemed cruel.

Adam Baker dropped out of the fourth grade the following week. He found a job stacking corrugated boxes at the end of an assembly line.

You advanced your queen-rook pawn one square.

"How does that move fight for these four squares?" Clarence the third asked.

"I don't know."

He sat back again in his chair. "Don't be afraid to fight," he said. "My father is using you. Don't let him do it."

"What should I do?"

"What do you think you should do?"

"I think I should quit."

"When did you get that idea?"

"When he first mentioned not paying me."

"Why didn't you quit then?"

"I was trying to be a nice guy."

"Being a nice guy doesn't mean spreading you cheeks. If anybody tries to spread your cheeks, break their nose for them."

"Should I hit the reverend?"

"Certainly not. In this case, quitting would be tantamount to breaking his nose for him."

"If I quit, I won't get to come over to learn chess."

"Playing chess has nothing to do with cleaning the house."

"You'll teach me even if I quit?" you asked.

"I won't teach you if you *don't* quit," he said. "One other thing, don't tell my father that I told you to quit. He might put me out."

As you were leaving, Marvin Abercrumbie was coming in the front vestibule door. He looked right past you at Clarence the third standing in the apartment doorway.

"Hey, man," he said walking by you, "you got my shit?"

"Of course," Clarence the third said closing the apartment door behind Marvin as he walked in.

Even with the door closed, you could still hear what was being said.

"This batch is some good stuff," Clarence said, "so I'll have to charge you a little extra."

"No matter," Marvin said, "I'll take it."

Since Big Ma ended the deal between you and the church the following Sunday, you were spared the agony of having to quit outright. But that didn't matter. By the next weekend, Clarence the third was gone anyway. Mrs. Higgins said that he had gone to New York to study chess under some grand master. Reverend Higgins only comment was, "Good-bye and good riddance."

XI

"Does God love Satan?"

"What kind of question is that?"

"What do you mean 'what kind of question is that?' It's a question question."

"It's a bullshit question."

"You're just afraid of what derives from the answer."

"I ain't scared of nothing."

"Then give me the answer."

"I don't know the answer."

"Ok, then, *I'll* give *you* the answer."

"What is the answer?" you ask.

"Yes." Phyllis removes the ice bag from your ankle and begins applying an elastic bandage.

You take the bait. "God cannot love Satan," you say.

"I knew you would say that," Phyllis smiles sweetly. "But you said it yourself. God *is* love. Therefore, God cannot *not* love. Therefore, God loves Satan."

"I also said that Satan is a fallen angle."

"I hope you're not suggesting that God denies him love because he is fallen."

"Well," you can hear the uncertainty in your voice, "yes."

Phyllis' smile fades a little. "You're so easy," he says. He finishes the ankle and moves to the elbow. "We are all fallen," he says. "None of us are wise."

He looks you in the eye, and for the first time you can almost see an innocence there, an almost child like quality.

He cleans the gash on your elbow with alcohol, and slaps a bandage on it. "You should have both of these X-rayed." Then he says, "If he denies Satan love, he denies us all love."

"We are His children."

"Satan is His son."

"Satan is competing with God for our loyalty."

"Only because God allows it."

"God *doesn't* allow it."

"At the very least, it is with God's tacit consent." Phyllis continues, "I would argue that it is with God's explicit consent, in fact, according to God's plan. But that might be more than you can handle."

"Don't fuckin' talk down to me."

He puts his medical supplies away, and wipes the table. "I talked to the big bazooka today."

"What did you say?"

"Nothing. It's what he said."

"Ok, what did *he* say?"

"He wants to come back."

"Do you want him back?"

"I don't know. I told him I had someone new." He looks at you carefully to measure your response.

"This is awkward," you say.

"I thought you would appreciate the beauty in this."

You ponder a moment. "Do you want me to leave?"

"No."

"You can't be asking for a commitment," you say. "What happened to honesty?"

"I want both."

"You can't have both. There is no 'Shanti and Phyllis. We hardly know each other."

Phyllis pauses a moment. "He said something else. Something about the case."

"What?!"

"Simply that there has been a serious new development."

"What is it?!" you ask again.

"He didn't say."

"Bullshit! Tell me what he said."

"What was it."

You pound the table once hard with your fist, "Damn." You want to stand up and storm out, but your ankle hurts too much. "Are you being straight with me?"

"I never lie," he says.

You push yourself up from the table. "I've got to talk to Jean." You say, "when did you talk to the bazooka?"

"This morning," he answers. "That's where I was when you woke up."

You use the cell phone to call Jean, and tell her to meet you at a rest stop on the road out of town. You hobble out to the car. As you pull away from the curb, you notice a car parked not far behind you with a person that looks a lot like Detective Middleman sitting in it. You pull up to the light at the corner, and signal a right turn. You look both ways, and turn on red. You're heading for the expressway. There are so many questions you have to ask Jean, and you have to look her in the eye when she answers. Lawyers have a way of lying even when they don't have to. This time you need the truth. What exactly did she find out at the police station? Who said what to whom? You need details. You need to know if she knows anything about a big break in the case.

As you approach the expressway, the car with the Middleman look-alike is a couple of cars behind you. That couldn't be him for real, could it? You pull onto the entry ramp and hit the gas to merge. You quickly cruise over to the fast lane, pass a couple of cars, then pull into the lane on the right and slow way down.

The car behind you makes the exact same maneuver. But when you pull to the right, you make sure there isn't enough room for him to pull in behind you. His momentum carries him almost up even with you. You look over quickly. It *is* Middleman. Where's Jack? You dart into the lane to the right, and floor it. This lane is clear for a ways, and you are able to put some distance between you and him. The traffic breaks up, and there is a long space between the pack of cars you're leading, and the pack ahead of you. You press the pedal hard. As you approach the pack ahead of you, you can see Middleman breaking out of the pack behind you. He's closing in.

Off in the distance, the road curves wide to the left. There is a large wooded area on the right, and farm land on the left. A house and barn and silo sit off in the middle of the field. The house is flanked by small clumps of trees.

Near the horizon, you can see traffic on the median strip. There are three police cars with red and blue flashing lights chasing another guy in your direction. The ground in the median must be bumpy, because the guy being chased is bouncing almost out of control. To stabilize his ride, he pulls onto the shoulder of the oncoming traffic. You hit your brakes, and the brake lights on all the cars ahead of you immediately go on. Somebody in the pack loses control, and swerves to the right. The car two cars ahead of you swerves to the left to avoid hitting him in the rear, and swerves directly into the path of the police chase. All you can hear is screeching rubber. The two cars crash head on so hard, that they bounce straight into the air about fifteen feet. The sound of crushing steel and breaking glass on impact puts a lump in your stomach, because you know no one could have survived the hit.

Right before your eyes, the order that was traffic flips into chaos. Cars are hitting each other and spinning out of control leaving glass and twisted debris in their wake. The pickup truck directly in front of you crashes into one of the two cars that crashed head on. As he hits, the rear of the truck rises up high enough for you to see everything from the front axle to the muffler. You are pressing the brakes as hard as you can, but you feel as if the car is not slowing down at all. You can hear your own wheels crying to stop, but the car feels like it is on ice. As the truck ahead of you begins to come back down, your fear is that you will slide under it and be crushed. You are squeezing the steering wheel with all your strength. The truck slams down missing your car by about six inches. Still sliding forward and swerving to the right, it slides into the next lane, and clips the car beside you. That car swerves into a concrete embankment. The truck spins enough for you to see the kid that was driving. He's about nineteen, and he is dead. The grill is crushed next to the windshield. The engine is sitting in his lap. His truck slides off to the right and rolls into a ditch.

All of a sudden, the road ahead of you is clear. The chaos continues in your rearview mirror. Middleman is taken out by a wheel flying into his windshield. It crushes the glass on the passenger side forcing him to lose control. His car swerves to the left, then to the right and spins around. The car is facing the opposite direction. He pulls off the road. You take your foot off the brake, and ease it over to the gas.

"You little dick sucking prick! He was out there waiting for me."

"No," Phyllis says. "We didn't talk about you. He didn't know you were here."

"You're a lie," you say. "I'm getting the fuck out of here."

"Don't go," he says. "You are safe here. I swear."

"Now can I trust you? You led him straight here."

"No, I didn't."

"Then why was he here? How did he know how to find me."

"Maybe he didn't. Maybe finding you here was a lucky break."

"You mean . . .."

"You got it smart guy."

"I don't want maybe," you say.

"Maybe is all there is."

"Bullshit!" You say, "some things are certain."

"If certainty existed, there would be no need for faith."

"You are so full of shit," you say.

"So name something that is certain."

"That I cannot trust you."

"But you can."

"How can I?"

"Judge me by my actions."

"What actions?"

"By what I did this morning."

"Ok, I'll bite."

"I went to tell the bazooka that I never wanted to see him again."

"Why did you tell him that?"

"It was a leap of faith."

"To what end?"

"I don't know," he says. "That is the essence of faith."

"You're an idiot! You can't have me. So by cutting him loose, you have nothing."

"It is not certain that I cannot have you."

"*That* part *is* certain."

He looks at you as you arrange the stoneyness in your face for emphasis. He blinks once and slowly smiles. "So what are you going to do?"

You pause. "I have no options."

"You have two options. You can go or you can stay."

"What changes if I stay?"

"Nothing," he says. "If you stay, I will fix some food like the dutiful wife that I am."

". . . that you want to be."

"You pick your words, and I'll pick mine."

"And the bazooka?"

"He knows better than to bother you here. You see, he's still in the closet. He can't even send that flunky Jack, because even he doesn't know that Arnie is gay."

"And if I go?"

"You'll be gone."

You ponder a moment. Then you say, "I hate this."

He says, "I'll slip into something nice."

XII

Everybody called him Lee Jack. His name was Leroy Jack Johnson. And like his name sake, he was buff, cut and powerful. During gym class, he would pose in front of the mirror admiring his pectorals and biceps. In the pool, he would pose on the diving board tensing his muscles before executing a perfect swan or jackknife. During fencing practice, he looked like Errol Flynn or Basil Rathbone or somebody. He was the one who showed you how to punch.

Her name was Trudy Miller. She was light-skinned with long hair and big legs. She was in your class, and she was one of the ones who people referred to as 'fast.' You had a secret crush on her. One day in the library, she told you that she was afraid to ask a question. She wanted to know if you would ask it for her. Naturally, you agreed. You raised your hand. The teacher, a stately looking woman, was a substitute. She didn't know any of the children by name, so the protocol she established was that she would point to the student who was to speak next. She pointed to you. "What is an iris?" you asked on Trudy's behalf. You knew the answer, but you asked anyway just to be of service to her.

The teacher answered the question, and Trudy rubbed your hand and thanked you profusely. She actually touched you. She was close enough for you to smell. The second question was, "What is a tibia?" This one you did not know. But again, the answer brought a touch from Trudy and a flash of her magic smile.

You raised your hand a third time. "What is a hymen?" The class fell silent, and all eyes turned to you. Everybody knew that you did *not* know.

Trudy was Lee Jack's girl. The next day in gym, the class was running laps. Lee Jack bumped into you. You thought it was on purpose, so you pushed him back. He squared off and punched you in the stomach. The air inside you gushed from your mouth as you doubled over. You could see the muscles in his left arm flexing as he drew back and punched you in the side. Gagging for air, your gaze fixed on the muscles in his legs sliding like machine parts under his skin as he shifted his weight to punch you in the other side, you heard him mumble, "that's for talking to Trudy."

Still airless, you collapsed to your knees on the floor. The color in the image of Lee Jack standing over you began fade. You slumped over hitting you shoulder and head on the gym floor. His image turned white like an overexposed photograph. Then, his image was gone.

* * *

"I'm though bending over," you said.

"The fuck you are," Reggie countered.

By now, Reggie was a grown man. You were thirteen, but big for your age.

"In fact, I'm fucking you right now. Take your shit off."

Resignation and resolve come in many forms. That was the lesson you learned three days after Clarence the third left town. It happened right in front of the church. That corner had no stop signs. Cars routinely barreled through that intersection without looking. That corner was an accident waiting to happen, and it happened that day.

It was a Dodge pickup truck and an old Chevy. The truck was going south, the Chevy west. And the hit itself wasn't bad. Barely a fender bender. The truck broadsided the Chevy after skidding on the brakes about ten feet. The impact was light enough that the Chevy barely moved. In fact, the guy in the Chevy pulled over to the side of the road. He got out on the passenger side and walked around to inspect the damage. He was a young black guy wearing khaki pants and a white t-shirt.

The guy in the truck, a portly white guy balding on top, had a problem. He looked around at all the black people standing and watching, and decided it wouldn't be safe to get out. After all, it was he who had hit the other guy. He tried to restart the truck. You could hear the fan grazing against something as the starter turned. He jerked his body forward as he spat "goddamnit" into the steering wheel. He pumped the gas and tried again. Smoke began to waft from beneath the hood. His expression changed. Now he smiled because he knew he had to get out and be friendly. He pulled the door handle, but the door wouldn't move. The impact of the hit was just enough to push the fenders back far enough that the doors wouldn't open. The smoke grew thicker. His expression changed again. His brow was pinched as the seriousness of the problem began to dawn on him. He put his shoulder to the door to no avail. An orange glow formed in the smoke, and soon, flames began to lick at the corners of the engine compartment. He began to panic. He looked around wildly. Smoke was pouring into the cabin. He slid to the other side and tried to force that door open. It, too, was stuck. He kicked the door. He hit the windows with his fists. He kicked the windows. The Chevy driver and a couple of other guys ran over and tried to open the doors from the outside. One guy got a crowbar. But before he could get the bar wedged into the crack between the door and the truck body, the engine burst into flames. Everybody backed away.

That's when you saw it. He knew he was trapped. He knew he was going to die. Standing on your porch, you could see straight into the front of the truck. He hit the steering wheel with his fist, then sat back. He turned his head just slightly, and looked you in the eye. Tears welled up in his eyes and streamed down his cheeks. He was sweating. Smoke filled the cabin. He didn't want to die, and he didn't want to look like a coward. He hit the window with his fist again and again and again. His head fell back. You could smell the tires burning. There was a sound like the sound a pea makes as it leaves the shooter, only louder, and the whole truck was burning. You could see him sitting there, totally engulfed in flames. Now you could smell him. In the distance you could hear the scream of sirens.

Reggie grabbed you by the collar. "I'm gon' make you suck my dick."

You could feel the tears welling up in your eyes. You curled your fist as tightly as you could, and swung. You felt the cartilage snap under you blow. You could hear it, too. Blood gushed from both his nostrils, and he dropped to the floor. His eyes were glassy. His head weaved a little as if he had trouble controlling his neck muscles. "And you bet' not mess with my sister neither," you said. He sat up for a moment, then lolled over onto his side. After a while, he went to the bathroom and cleaned himself up.

When Big Ma got home, she asked him about it. "What happened to yo' face?"

"Aw, Ma," he said, "I fell down at work."

"You need to find a different job. One where you won't be falling down like that," she said.

XIII

Phyllis is as good as his word. He shops. He cooks. And he's right. He *is* a good cook. He fixes shit you usually get only in restaurants. He even makes his own mayonnaise. Sometimes you forget that mayonnaise doesn't just materialize in a jar somewhere ready for folks to buy. And you pay him for the food. He didn't want to take the money at first, using the ole I'm-not-a-prostitute argument. But when you pointed out to him that husbands often give wives an allowance, he relented. He liked the idea of you referring to yourself– albeit obliquely– as a husband, his husband.

The problem is that you were short of money. You only had a few dollars in your wallet when you bolted. So you need to get some cash.

"Remember this," Phyllis says. "ATM use is not anonymous."

"I'll drive to a mall in the suburbs."

You pick Northbrook. It's a good ways from the building. It's a good ways from Phyllis's. Nobody knows you in Northbrook. Nobody is looking for you in Northbrook. You can walk around like a normal person, like a person unknown to the police, like the innocent person you are.

Sometimes, until the weight is removed, you don't know you're carrying it. In Northbrook, the weight of being hunted is removed, and you feel as if your body stands a little bit straighter, a little bit stronger. The feeling is so palpable, you can play with it. One moment, you can imagine being back at the building, and the weight returns. In the next moment, you can look around at the stores, the mannequins decked out to here, the people decked out like mannequins, and the weight is gone again. You stride is lighter, surer, freer.

"'Shanti!"

That can't be for you. Nobody knows you out here.

"'Shanti!"

The call is closer now. You don't want to turn around, because you don't want to acknowledge your name. Acknowledging it makes you vulnerable, visible, known. Your hope is that the person is calling someone else with the same name. Somebody. Anybody. Just not you.

The woman's voice is right behind you now. "Boy, you better stop ignoring me like that."

Damn! You spin around. It's Pat Simpson, clown face and high heels. "Pat," you say. "I didn't know it was you."

"And you didn't bother to turn around to see if it was me."

"I'm sorry," you say.

"So how you been? I hear you're on the lam."

You don't remember Pat being so forthright. "I've been away for a couple of days."

"I'm President of the Board now."

"How do you like it?"

"I like it a lot. Ha!" She says, "I should have been president a long time ago. Now I can buy stuff for the building. Wallpaper. Carpet. Plants. Earl was so cheap."

"That's what Sean always said."

"He's here with me, by the way." She looks around as if wondering where he is. And as if on queue, he comes into view from among a small group of people like a ghost from among the trees. He has a large shopping bag in each hand.

"'Shanti," he says. "My friend! I just wish I had had the nerve to do it."

"Oh, hush up, Sean. 'Shanti didn't hurt that boy."

"Well, somebody did it. I was just hoping it was somebody I knew."

"It still might be," you answer. "It's just not me."

"I'm going to give you a word of advice," Pat says to me, "expect the unexpected."

"What do you mean?"

"I'm not sure. I went down to the laundry room the night Earl got hurt, and I peeked into the office. It was a few minutes before midnight. The door was closed. But I saw the light on, so I opened it and looked in. Earl gave me the funniest look."

"Look?"

"Yeah, like he had been caught playing with himself," she said. "I was so taken aback, that I looked to see whether or not he *had* been playing with himself."

"Had he?" Sean asked, clearly hoping the answer was yes.

"No, but he was hiding something."

"Any clue what?" you ask.

"No, but it was small enough for him to cup in his hand or along his arm."

What could Earl have possibly been hiding? "Did you say anything to him?"

"I just said something like 'oh, it's you.' He smiled a funny grin, and I went on to do my laundry."

"How close to midnight was it?" you ask.

"About ten to."

"Was he alone?"

"Yes."

The time line is funny. She saw him alone at ten to, and at five to, you got the mystery call. It had to have been him. You strain to remember what the voice sounded like, but it's already beginning to fade. It said, "come down to the office." But what was the tone? What else did it say? Was he hurt already? The window was only five minutes, but someone else could have come it.

Sean complains about the bags being heavy, and they hurry off. You get your money and leave. This place doesn't feel safe anymore.

A couple of day later, you call Jean. She doesn't answer. You cruise by the building just to see if the cops are still around. They appear to be gone. You go in and ring Alice's bell. She buzzes you in. You take the stairs to her floor.

She's in the bathroom again. "I'll be out in a minute," she says.

Alice's place looks different than it did three years ago. Of course, maybe you didn't really look three years ago. But now the drapes are open, and the morning light was pouring in. The computer in the corner looks new. The shelves of books don't look new, but they don't look familiar.

You move to the hallway to see if you can see into the bedroom. The door is closed, but not all the way. You tiptoe closer. You don't want Alice to know that you are snooping. You ease the door open to look around. The unmade bed is where you remember it. The sheets are different; the bedspread is the same. The dresser is in the same place as well. You remember the oblong mirror with the rounded corners. Reflected in the mirror, you can see a half-naked woman standing in the shadows in the walk-in closet across the room. Her back is to you, but she looks familiar. It's her hair. From the back, she looks a lot like Jean.

Just then, Alice pops out of the bathroom. You spin around to face her.

"I'm sorry," you mumble, "I just wanted to see . . .."

At the same moment the woman in the closet turns to face you. It *is* Jean.

"What are *you* doing here," you ask.

She doesn't answer. You look around at Alice. Alice looks you straight in the eye and raises one eyebrow. Then she cocks her head to one side, squares her shoulders and walks right past you into the bedroom. She sashays directly into the walk-in closet and stands next to Jean. Looking you straight in the eye again, she puts her arm around Jean's waist, and pulls her close. Jean is stiff at first, almost reluctant. Alice leans over and kisses her in the mouth. Jean stiffens even further. Slowly, she begins to relax. After a few seconds, she melts into Alice's embrace. Then she begins to warm up. She switches the angle of the kiss, and puts her tongue full into Alice's mouth. Now Alice begins to stiffen. This is apparently further than Alice had planned to go right now. But Jean is not to be denied. She steps back a step, removes her panties, the only piece of clothing she is wearing, and hops onto the bed, pulling Alice behind her.

Jean is half a head shorter than Alice. So it seems incongruous to you to see Jean taking the lead. She directs Alice to lie face up. Alice does. Then Jean, resting on her knees, straddles Alice's face, and rocks her pussy back and forth in her mouth. You can nearly smell the pussy from across the room. Jean comes and groans. She unbuttons and unzips the pants Alice is wearing, and pushes them down along Alice's thighs. Alice raises her hips to help the process. After Jean pushes the pants past her knees, Alice kicks them off and spreads her knees. Jean rubs Alice's already wet pussy with her finger tips. Alice wraiths in pleasure, arching her back. Jean pushes her two middle fingers in as far as they will go, and works them in and out. Alice comes and moans, and you can hear her pussy begin to smack. Now Jean pushes her index finger in, too. The hair around Alice's pussy is matted with come. You wonder if she has a yeast infection. Jean adds her little finger to the other three. She plunges all four fingers in and out of Alice's pussy like a piston. Those little worker hands that she thinks of as chicken claws. You remember how they looked the first night you met her, sitting on the floor fingering a G chord, bony and white with tendons protruding at the back. The expression on Jean's face looks now like it did then, determined, almost mean, a woman at work. With the agility of a wrestler, she spins off of Alice's face and straddles one of Alice's legs. Still resting most of her weight on her knees, she cradles Alice's leg like a big Teddy bear. She slides the toes of both her feet underneath Alice's ankle. Alice's mouth and chin and cheeks are moist with come. As if she knows what is next, Alice braces herself. Her hands clutch at the sheet at both edges of the bed. Her free foot is planted firmly on the bed, and her pussy is angled up. Jean tucks in her thumb, and pushes her whole hand into Alice's pussy. You're stunned! You couldn't imagine a woman's pussy would open so wide without her being pregnant. Alice's body tightens as she lifts her hips off the bed. Alice's pussy lips are pink around Jean's wrist. The muscles in Jean's forearm flex. You reckon she must be making a fist inside her. Alice's body relaxes as Jean moves her fist gently to and fro.

You approach the bed slowly, and put your hand on Jean's back. Still stroking Alice, she looks up at you.

"I want some, too," you tell her.

"Of course," she says, "please, come inside." She arches her back to expose her pussy.

You remove your pants and straddle Alice's outstretched leg as you scoot up to Jean's ass. You rub Alice's thigh with both hands, then you rub Jean's thighs. Their skin is noticeably different. Jean's skin is soft, but Alice's skin is soft in a different way. You slide your dick deep into Jean's pussy. You can feel you testicles and rectum rubbing over Alice's leg. You reach around with both hands and fondle Jean's tits. You move one hand to Alice's thigh, and you rub up around her butt. Jean is still stroking her slowly. You slide your fingers over Alice's rectum. It is wet with come. You go to slide you finger into Alice's butt.

"No," Jean says, "no! You can't fuck her!"

"What's up with that?" you say. "You two put on this super sexy show in front of me, and then tell me I can't have any?"

"You *can* have some," Jean says. "You can have me."

"I want you both," you demand.

"Listen, guys," Alice says, "this is not the time for a family argument."

"You are my man, and I don't want you to fuck her."

"You are my woman and my lawyer," you counter, " and I didn't want *you* to fuck her. But you already have. So now what?"

"I don't want to loose you," Jean says.

"You won't loose me," you tell her. "I'm yours even after I fuck her. It is, after all, only sex."

"You might like her pussy better than mine."

"Better pussy does not a better relationship make," you tell her.

"Besides," Alice says, "he's not my type. The three of us can be fuck buddies, but that's it. So now can we get back to it."

"You be quiet," Jean says. "You just want him to fuck you."

"I just don't think it's fair to tease him," Alice says. "I mean, you did start this in front of him."

"I didn't start this," Jean says, "you kissed me first."

"Yeah," Alice counters, "but I hadn't planned on eating you with him around. And I certainly was *not* going to take my clothes off. Like him, I thought everything was fair game when you took my pants off."

"Take your hand out," you tell Jean. She does. "Now crawl on top of Alice." She hesitates. "Do it," you say. Her eyes grow watery. She sniffs, then brushes the tears away.

With you still in her, Jean crab walks onto Alice's body. To keep from slipping out, you walk on your knees behind her. Alice puts her arms around Jean's neck; Jean slides her arms under Alice's armpits, and cradles her shoulders. Alice comforts her. "It's ok," she says, "it won't mean a thing." They kiss deeply. Alice lifts and spreads her knees to offer up her pussy. You push into Jean a few times, then you slide out of her and push deep into Alice. Her pussy is not as tight as Jean's. She's a little deeper, too. She rocks her pelvis up to meet you. You push in, barely getting to the back. You don't remember her pussy being this big. Having just had Jean's whole arm inside her probably didn't help. You rub her legs, then you rub Jean's legs. You reach around and fondle both sets of breasts along the sides. You can't reach the nipples. You slide out of Alice and back into Jean. You stroke four times and switch, four times and switch, four times and switch. You're in Alice now. This switching back and forth isn't working. Any build up towards an orgasm is lost during the switch. So you slide out of Alice, and position the head of your dick between both pussies. Using short, steady strokes you bring them both to near orgasm. Then Jean comes. You reach around and rub Jean's pussy with your fingers. She keeps coming as you sink you dick into Alice. Alice comes. Then you come in Alice. For one magic moment, all of you are coming at the same time. You wonder if this is what it is like to be a pimp. Alice and Jean cling to each other and rub each other.

You open your eyes, and they're still there. You are in the spoon position behind Jean; Alice is in the spoon position behind you. You're reaching around fondling Jean's tits; Alice is reaching around fondling your nuts. Feeling your dick getting hard, she scoots under the cover and puts it in her mouth. You can feel her rubbing her tongue over the slit. Her technique is good, but not and good as Phyllis's.

There's no talking now, just shifting bodies. Everybody knows what to do. Jean begins to stir as she feels you stirring. You shift her hips up toward your head, and she knows you want to eat her. She sits on your face just as she had earlier sat on Alice's. She rocks to and fro, her rectum bumping your nose. You can feel as she reaches over to fondle Alice's face as Alice sucks your dick. Then she gestures for Alice to shift around so Jean can eat her. Alice shifts around, Jean lies to one side in order to get to Alice's pussy, you shift over to keep eating Jean. It's spontaneous and it's perfect. The three of you form a triangle on the bed. You're eating Jean; Jean is eating Alice; Alice is eating you. No one is coming now. You're all simply in the zone fucking.

Presently, you ease you dick out of Alice's mouth. You scoot to your knees, and switch around. You put your dick in Jean's pussy and your tongue in Alice's mouth. Then Alice shifts around and puts her pussy in your mouth. She sits up. You roll onto your back and Jean follows you until she is straddling your hips with your dick still inside her.

Alice says to you, "This is called a Feast of Peonies. Do you like it?" She rubs her pussy hard on your face, then comes in your mouth. Her fluid has a delicate saltiness to it, and the taste of it makes your dick seem to get harder, which, in turn, you push deeper into Jean, and she comes, too. A pussy on your dick, and a pussy in your mouth. You feel like Superman. A feast of peonies! Two beautiful flowers! Suddenly, the image of Superman plucking and eating red and pink flowers flashes into your mind, and you chuckle into Alice's pussy. Then, just as suddenly, another thought comes to mind. A question really. How come? How come you? Every man on earth wants this, but you got it. How come? Is there a reason? It's not like you went after it, planned it out, worked the plan, and bingo! No. You stumbled into it. You didn't even as much as conceive the notion. Yet, here it is. The bossest sex you've ever had in your life. So why here? Why now? Why you? Is it luck? Some folks would call it luck. Some folks would call you a degenerate. But fuck 'em. Fuck that people think. This is the bossest sex in the world, a pussy at both ends, and people think you're a freak if you want it. Fuck 'em! People will think anything.

So why Phyllis? He gives good head, but his ass ain't as good as this. People would think you're a freak for fucking him. But fucking Phyllis don't make you no punk. In a way, Phyllis ain't no punk. It took balls to walk into the Latin Club dressed like that. It took balls to put the dress on in the first place! But he had the courage to do it. Is that why God sent him to that faggot priest in the first place? To give him courage? He wanted to be God's instrument, but God's instrument fucked him in the ass. Did the priest have courage? Did Reggie?

Jean shifts, and now she is sucking you dick. Her technique is rougher, but it, too, falls short of Phyllis's. After about twenty minutes of this, you roll over sated.

"You know, guys," you say, "I came to pick up some of my stuff. I don't know how we got so sidetracked into this."

"Your stuff is at my place," Jean says. Her voice is mechanical. She pulls herself up slowly to get dressed. "I'll get it for you."

She pulls on Alice's panties and pants and bathrobe. She closes the front door behind her.

After a few moments, you ask, "How long have you two been seeing each other?" That expression again!

"Only this last week or so," she answers.

"So how did it go down?"

"Well," she says, "you know we have been friends for a long time."

You didn't know it, but you nod your head yes.

"She stopped by last week because I had called her and told her that I needed to talk. That's what we do. Even living in the same building, we might not see each other for months. But then one of us will call the other, and we will sit up until three in the morning talking girl talk. She usually complains about work. I usually rant about being alone. She came by, and as soon as she walked in, I began to cry. I don't know what happened after that. She hugged me and kissed me on the cheek, and the next thing I knew, we were kissing for real. Then she had my t-shirt and bra off and was sucking my breasts, and I was liking it. It all went so fast. She had a dildo in her pocket. I don't know where she got that thing, but it was wonderful. It was just what I needed. She knew my need, and she was there for me." She pauses a moment, then asks, "Are you done?"

"Almost," you answer. You move closer to her and put your hand between her legs. "I want to put my hand in you."

"It's not going to work," she says pulling her knees up to her chest and spreading them wide. "Jean has small hands, and her wrist is only a little bigger than your cock. Your hand is too big."

You push your middle two fingers into her, and work them around. She isn't as wet now, and you can tell the friction is uncomfortable to her. You try to put your index finger in, too, but she closes her knees.

"Stop." She says, "you're hurting me."

"Open your legs," you tell her.

"But you're hurting me," she whines.

"Then go get some of that jelly stuff."

She gets up and fetches a tube of lubricating gel from the bathroom. She walks back to the bed slathering it on her pussy.

"That's better," she says lying back down. "Now let's try it again."

Lying aslant her body, you push your middle two fingers into her again in order to spread the gel all the way around. Then you add your index finger. There is less friction, but the squeeze is tight. You force them in. You can feel her flesh expanding. She catches her breath, and writhes. You don't know if it is from pleasure or pain. You don't care which it is. You never realized how satisfying it was to put so much of your hand into a woman's pussy. You take your hand out and, sliding the rest of the way onto her body, you stuff your barely hard dick in. You can't do it. It hurts, and it is tired. You roll off and lapse into a dream.

You're underwater swimming. You must be in a large aquarium, because the light overhead is bright like flourescent tubes. There are Angel fish swimming around you, but they ignore you. They must think you are a fish, too. Then Tiger Barbs attack you, nipping at your fingers and toes. It isn't painful, just annoying. They make it hard for you to move through the water. Sounds in the water echo. There's a thump, thump, thump. You look around, and you can see Phyllis knocking on the glass to scare the Barbs off you. Thump, thump, thump. You're awakened by a knock at the door and a voice.

"It's the police. Open up."

Alice hops up and scrambles to get something on. You grab your clothes and run to the bathroom. Why did they think you were a fish? She opens the door. "Can I help you, officer," she says.

"Where . . . is he?"

You recognize Middleman's voice and his theatrical cadence.

"Where is who?" Alice asks.

"Don't dally with me."

"I assure you, officer," she says, "the last thing I want to do is dally with you."

"Then tell me where he is before I have to come in and tear this place up."

"He's probably in the bathroom." Its Jean's voice.

"Do you have a warrant?" Alice asks.

"I don't need a warrant."

Having dressed yourself, you step out of the bathroom. You're no hero, but you know cops think nothing of tearing a place up if they have to, even a little shit like Middleman who is standing in the center of the livingroom wearing a neck brace. It looked like a piece of ice around his neck, cold, white, clean, new. Why couldn't he have died like that young kid in the truck?

"Ashanti Ra," he says, then pauses, "I am arresting you for the attempted murder of Earl Gilbert."

"Attempted murder?" you ask.

"He didn't die," he says, "and you are the one he fingered."

That must be the new development you heard about. "He's lying."

"It's your word against his."

You think quickly. "So," you say, "have you talked to Phyllis lately." The Barbs are nipping at you.

"Leave Phillip out of this."

"You should talk to her."

"*He* doesn't want to talk to me."

"She'll talk if I tell her to." You don't wait for him to respond. You pick up the phone and dial the number.

"Who is Phyllis?" Jean asks.

Alice shrugs.

"Phyllis, baby, I got a problem. The big bazooka just arrested me. Talk to him."

You hand the phone to Middleman. His whole demeanor changes, especially his voice. His voice is higher, more effeminate. He turns his back on the three of you to try to get some privacy. "Hi, Phil." Alice and Jean stare at his back in complete disbelief, their mouths hanging open. Seeing your opportunity, you slip out of the door, and bump smack into Jesus. You bounce off of each other like two Sumo wrestlers.

"Shit," he says. You hope and expect him to lapse into silence. But he sees that it is you. "Shanti," he says. "I was just looking for you." Has talking become his new vocation?

"Shhh," you say, "I can't talk now." You step to your right, and he steps to his left to get your attention. You step to your left, and he steps to his right. "Damnit, Jesus, I have to go."

"I want to thank you, man."

"Thank me later." You slip by him.

Just then, Middleman bounds out of the door and runs right into Jesus just as Jesus is turning his body to let you through. The force of the collision knocks Middleman against the wall. He bounces off and freezes. The pain in his neck stops him dead in his tracks. He looks at you backing towards the elevator, but he can't even speak. You push the button to go down.

The elevator doors open. You duck in and push the button for the lobby.

"Shanti."

It's Sean.

"Fancy seeing you again."

"I can't talk now," you say.

"I know, I know. Just be careful."

The elevator doors open at the ground floor. You're just about to dash out when it occurs to you that Middleman might not be alone.

"Sean, can you . . .?"

"Sure, buddy," he says, "I'll check for you." He looks like a buzzard leaning over to see without being seen. "There's someone in the front lobby."

"What does he look like?"

"Well, he doesn't live in this building."

"Like a poster boy for the Marines?"

"Yeah!"

Shit! "Do you have your storage room key?"

He gives it to you. You tell him you will leave it on the windowsill by the north lockers. By now, the elevator doors are trying to close, and you have to hold them open with your foot. The warning buzzer goes off, and the doors begin to force themselves close. The two of you step off.

Jack has just been buzzed in the inside lobby door, and he sees you fumbling with the storage room key. "Stop that man," he shouts to Sean.

Sean shrugs and puts his hands in the air. The gesture implies that he's not getting involved. Jack runs up the couple of stairs from the lobby floor to the main landing. You open the storage room door, slip in, and slam it behind you. Jack is outside pounding to get in. You limp for the window. You can hear Jack asking Sean if he has a key. You hear a smack and Jack demanding Sean to give him the key.

You crawl out the window just like before. This time, instead of lowering yourself as far as you can then letting go, you lower yourself at the very edge of the door and use the cracks in the bricks of the garage wall to create friction against your body as you fall. It works only marginally. You still hit the ground pretty hard, but you don't damage you ankle any further. Sugar Baby would not have approved.

You hobble back to the car as fast as your ankle will let you, and drive straight back to Phyllis' place.

"The bitch turned me in! My own lawyer!"

"He was really pissed when you left," Phyllis says.

"Why would she do that?"

"He says you humiliated him."

You pause a moment. "She did it to get even."

"For what?"

"For not loving her."

"Do you care to flesh that out any?"

"We had an argument the night you and I met. She wanted to know when we were getting married. I laughed. I almost laughed in her face. The woman lies too much. She lives that lawyer shit day and night, like a politician. She has a real problem with honesty."

"Don't we all," he says.

"I told her she had great pussy, but that I didn't love her in that way. Boy, was that the wrong thing to say. She said something about being good enough to fuck but not good enough to marry. I tried to clean it up, but she was right. I thought she was good enough to fuck but not good enough to marry. She felt like shit and cried. I felt like shit and went out to get drunk. I went to the Latin Club. The rest is history."

"A woman scorned and all of that," he said.

"Yes, and all of that."

"So now what?"

"It's over."

"And?" He looks at you with eyes blinking with mock innocence. "Am I your only woman now?"

You look to the right, then to the left, then to the right again. "Don't do this to me, Phyllis."

"Do what?" He is sitting on the floor at your feet.

"Why couldn't you be a real woman?"

"I *am* a real woman."

Minutes before Big Ma died, she told you something. She said, in substance, it's a funny thing about death. You fear it all your life. You hear stories about it. You talk about it at parties. But looking at it standing there looking back at you, the first thought that hits you is, why me? Why is it my turn? Is this really the way it goes down? And in a split second, you process about a hundred thoughts at one time. The first one is a wonder. Could you have avoided this moment? Did you see it coming? Why now? Why here? Why this way? How does it fit into the whole scheme of things? Could you have done a better job of living this life?

The second one is coming to grips with it. It's not so bad. It's no worst than falling off a bicycle. The moment happens so quickly, you almost don't have time to fear it. You only fear it when it isn't there.

The last one consists of looking around at the setting as if somehow it is important to memorize the event. As if memorizing it will somehow preserve your life, will somehow give your life added meaning. But it doesn't help. The search for meaning in life is a curse on mankind because there is no meaning. Life simply is what it is. The meaning it has is the meaning we give it. The strongest don't always survive, and the best ideas don't always win out. In fact, they rarely do. Those that survive are those that are picked to survive. Those that win are those that are picked to win. How do you measure best anyway when it comes to ideas? The search for the measure of best ideas ends in an ethical quagmire.

You think you should have planned your life better. Then you realize that more planning wouldn't help. You realize that you should have lived your life as if you were on the verge of dying at every moment. And in fact, you were. We all are. Life is like that. One moment after the next. And the next. And the next. Until they run out. And make them count! It shouldn't be *Carpe diem*, seize the day. It should rather be seize the moment. Seize the moment, and the day will take care of itself.

Phyllis moves to unzip your pants, but you stop him. Your dick is already tired. You cup his face in your hands, and you kiss him. You put your tongue deep into his mouth.

* * *

It's morning. The next morning. Phyllis is up already, and you can smell coffee brewing. You look at the picture of Mom looking out at you with those branding iron eyes. You look at young Phillip sucking his thumb looking up at her, and you look at Dad staring off at the guild frame. You look back at Mom, and for the first time you notice the hint of a smile on her lips. Her mouth is set, but the corners are turned up ever so slightly as if she is stifling a smile. And Dad is looking away to keep himself from breaking out into uproarious laughter. How come you never noticed that before? The background is blurry, but you can make out the peak of a roller coaster. This can't be Riverview! Phyllis isn't that old. You get up and shower and dress. You meander down to the kitchen. The table is set with fresh-cut flowers, fresh squeezed orange juice, blue berry pancakes, and a whole platter of bacon and sausages. You sit down at the table and begin munching a strip of bacon.

Phyllis comes around and pecks you on the lips. "Did you sleep well?"

"Like a baby," you answer.

He gives a self-satisfied chortle. You don't bother to tell him that it was not his love that knocked you out last night.

You grab another strip of bacon. "Earl didn't die."

"And?"

"And he told the bazooka that I was the one that did it."

"When did he do that?"

"I don't know," you answer, "maybe as soon as they got him to the hospital. Maybe the next day."

"There is something wrong with this scenario," he says turning pancakes on the griddle. "Why would he cut his own throat just to implicate you? And why has he been in there so long?"

"I don't know. Maybe he . . .."

"I'll bet he tried to kill himself and fucked it up."

"Wouldn't the bazooka know that?" you ask.

"Yes."

"I'll bet he's trying to get back at you for dumping him."

Phyllis poses for a moment with one hand on his hip. "That bastard."

"I need to talk to Earl," you say.

"No," he says, "you need to see his chart. He's at County, and I've got friends at County."

He reaches for the phone and dials some numbers. "Hi, girl," he says, "I need a favor." He tells whomever it is he is talking to what he wants. They put him on hold for a couple of minutes. Then he says um-hum a few times, nods a few times, then says, "Thanks, baby, 'bye." He turns to you, "We're out of luck. The chart is still in his room."

"What room is he in?" you ask.

"You're not going up there, are you?"

"The fuck I'm not."

"I'm coming, too. You won't know what to look for."

Along the way, you stop at a florist's and buy a huge bouquet of flowers, white lilies. You want it to look like you're being friendly, bringing flowers to an old buddy. Who knows? Maybe he'll fall for it. The two of you take the elevator to his floor and find his room. He's in the old building where they still have wards and what seems like fifty beds flanking a long aisle. You've been told many times over the years about the hard time your mother had delivering you here at Cook County Hospital, and you catch yourself trying to conger up a memory. An image comes to mind of your mother and father smiling down at you, and you realize that it's not a memory at all. Rather, it is the recollection of the image you always get upon hearing the story. Still, you look around for something familiar. Was it this drab back then?

You step into the ward and stop cold. Phyllis runs into the back of you.

"Damn, baby," he says, "what you do that for?"

You step back trying to hide behind the edge of the wall, glad now for its drabness hoping it well help you be unnoticed.

"Baby," he says, dancing around to keep from being stepped on, "what's up?"

"Middleman is in there."

"The bazooka?"

"He's talking to Earl. Shit!" you say.

Phyllis wants to take a look, but you push him back. "Don't look," you say, "I know it's him."

"We've got to do something," he says, "visiting hours will be over in a few minutes."

"Call him," you say. "Call him on the phone."

"You can't use a cell phone in here."

"Then find a fucking pay phone!"

Phyllis disappears around the bend towards the elevators.

Earl is about half way down the isle. His small body looks like that of a child under the sheet. The bandages at his throat are barely visible. Middleman is explaining something to him, making wide arm gestures. Finally, the phone by the bed rings. Listening to Middleman, Earl ignores it. On the fourth ring, he picks it up. He hands it to Middleman. There is a short conversation. Middleman checks his watch. He hangs up. Instead of leaving, though, he begins gesticulating with his hands again. He's still there when Phyllis comes up behind you.

"What did you say to him?" you ask.

"I told him there was an emergency on the first floor that he needed to deal with right away."

"He didn't buy it," you say.

"I'll fix that," he says walking over to a door marked 'Emergency Exit Only. Alarm Will Sound.' He pushes it open, and a siren sounds. You peek into the ward. Middleman is running towards you looking back over his shoulder at Earl. Earl spots you and tries to alert Middleman, but Middleman is turning towards you now. You duck behind a screen as Middleman races around the bend towards the elevators.

You step into the ward heading towards Earl. You don't know where he was hiding, but Phyllis is right behind you.

You know you need to be careful. Earl is already frantically pushing the buzzer for the nurse. You saw a tractor and trailer once that had hit a bridge over the highway. The clearance under the bridge was eleven feet. The trailer was thirteen feet high. The truck was carrying a load of steel rods and sheets, and it had to have been moving way over the speed limit. When it hit, the bridge didn't move. The truck stopped cold caught by the front edge of the trailer. The rods kept going. Six of them. They punctured the front wall of the trailer, the rear wall of the cab, and the driver who had just slammed into the steering wheel and was probably dead from that impact anyway. One of the rods went through the driver and crashed through the windshield. The person you were with said that the driver simply wasn't careful enough, that he forgot what he was hauling.

Earl looks up at you. "Oreo shit, aren't you in jail, yet?" He's still pressing the buzzer.

"I brought you some flowers."

"Keep your fucking flowers, and get the fuck out of here."

You drop the white lilies on his chest.

"You hoping for a funeral, you bastard," he says.

"I guess I knew you were disappointed with the way I voted, but this is a bit much."

"I said, get the fuck out!" He presses the buzzer even harder.

You look around to be sure no one else can hear you, then whisper through clenched teeth, "listen, you pathetic little shit. You don't know who the fuck you are messing with. I will hurt you more than you have already hurt yourself."

"I hate you," Earl says. "And get these flowers off me."

You see two nurses running down the aisle. You leave the flowers on his chest, and grab the clipboard at the foot of his bed. You head out of the ward. The clipboard is yanked from your hand by the brass chain tethering it to the bed. You grab the board up, snatch the charts from beneath the clip, and head out. Phyllis trails closely behind. The nurses block your way. Phyllis jumps between them and you, and pretends to stumble into them. In the split second you gain, you whip around them and out of the ward. Looking back, you can see that Earl wants to shout, but he can't. One of the nurses looks at you, but you brush him off by looking away. The other one rushes straight to Earl. You and Phyllis head for the staircase at the opposite end of the hall. But as you approach it, you can hear Middleman lumbering back up. Then Phyllis and you duck through the emergency door. You pull it behind you, but it won't close. You look around to see why. It's Maria Santos smiling sweetly at you.

"I really want to thank you for . . .."

You grab her and snatch her into the stairwell. "Not now, Maria." You slam the door, and the alarm stops.

Maria is wearing green scrubs. The shirt is huge and the pants are tiny. She's wearing shoes!

"You have made Jesus and me so happy."

You and Phyllis are bounding down the stairs. "Name your first child after me," you toss over your shoulder.

You can hear in her voice that she thinks it is a great idea. "We will," she says, "we will!"

On the main floor, a security guard shouts, "That's him! Search him."

They grab Phyllis. Looking the other way, you walk by with the file. As you approach the revolving door in the front of the building, the elevator doors open. You hear Middleman's voice, "Not him you idiots. *Him!*" You look over your shoulder. Middleman is pointing at you, and Phyllis has broken away towards you at a full run. Middleman can't chase him because of his neck.

You scramble through the front doors, and, because you're looking over your shoulder at Middleman, you run smack into someone. You feel yourself falling to the ground. Phyllis picks up the file and blasts off down the street. You recover quickly. You look over to see who you ran into so you can at least say you're sorry before running on. Oh, shit! It's Jack. You pick yourself up and head off in the other direction at top speed. The ankle hurts, but you run through the pain. Jack shakes his head clear. He sees that it is you, and scrambles up. He gives chase.

You run to the intersection and out into traffic. Jack is right behind you. You jump some hedges, and your injured ankle buckles. You hit the ground again. You can feel Jack over you so you roll back to your feet, and all in one motion, swing a right cross. You catch him on the side of the head, but you wrist folds, and the punch has little power. He's only stunned. You lunge for the alley, but Jack recovers too quickly. He grabs your sleeve. You swing wildly with your left, and miss.

"I told you it wasn't over," he says.

You're panting hard, and you can hardly spit it out. "Fuck you." You have got to get back in shape.

He hits you with a right over-hand punch. You sprawl into a garbage dumpster. He comes down beside you on one knee, and starts drilling you with his right hand. He jams you in the face about six times. You feel yourself fading out when you hear the pop. You know you've been shot; you just don't know where. You can't feel the burn of an entry wound. Who was it that told you being shot feels like scalding hot water? All you can feel is Jack's weight resting heavily on your chest. He must be sitting on you.

Then you hear a voice. "Wake up, baby, we got to go." It's Phyllis. He's trying to lift your shoulders off the ground. You look around, and see Jack lying on the ground, shielded by the dumpster, blood running from his ear, a lot of blood. There's a gun in the blood.

"What happened?" you ask.

"That's Arnie's gun. I told you I knew the combination."

You stand up wobbly. Phyllis dusts you off.

"We got to go," he says.

The two of you exit at the far end of the alley just as Middleman approaches the near end. You hobble around the corner to the car. He puts you in the passenger seat, and tosses the file in your lap. He starts the engine.

"So what does it say?" He can't keep the anxiety out of his voice.

You flip through the file.

"Here it is," you says. "'Multiple trial cuts before nicking the windpipe. No major blood vessels cut.' The doctor reckons it was a botched suicide."

"That's all we need," he says, "let's go home."

It's odd the way life leads a person around by the nose. It was never your intention to become a computer programmer. You started out wanting to write poetry like your parents. But the die was cast on the very first day of registration at the University of Illinois at Chicago. Back then, it was still called Chicago Circle. You were a veteran going to college on the G.I. bill, and the amount of money you received per month was determined by the number of class hours you enrolled. You had to enroll in at least twelve quarter hours in order to get the maximum benefit. That translated into at least four three-hour classes. The problem was that all the good English classes were already closed except by consent of the instructor. You had a small collection of poems and stories that you showed to a couple of the teachers hoping they would be good enough to gain you entree into the classes you wanted. It didn't work. The first instructor you showed your work to was polite. He was a tall man with horn rim glasses, baggy jeans and a tread-bare tweed sport jacket. His speech and hand gestures were precise as if they were all rehearsed. Is it possible that he knew the Bazooka?

"Your work lacks imagination," he had said.

His colleague, a frumpy woman in her forties who walked with a stoop and had what appeared to you to be beet-red skin and dandruff on her nose and cheeks, was less gracious. "You have about as much talent as a toad stool," she said, "*sans* the toad."

Naturally, you were crushed. As you stood waiting for the elevator just around the corner from Miss Frumpty-dumpty's office, you could hear her laughing into the telephone. She was probably talking to that pedantic clown with the corncob up his ass. "Fuck these folks," you murmured to yourself.

But you still had to register, and Formal Logic was open. In fact, only three students were signed up. As you signed your name to the roster, you could hear footsteps approaching behind you. They stopped just as you finished filling in your social security number. "Oh, wow," the woman behind you said. "Are we in luck or what?"

"Only four people signed up," the other one said. "This is going to be a great class."

"Ashanti," the first one said as she signed her name below yours. She was short and round with long blonde hair that reached nearly to her waist. "That is such a cool name."

"Is that your name?" the second one asked in near amazement. She was less short and less round. Her waist-length blonde hair wasn't really blonde, yet something about her smile made her feel like the friendlier of the two. The smile was genuine.

"That's my name," you answered.

"My name is Mary," the first one said. "She's Victoria."

"They call me Vicky."

"So are you two sisters or something?" you asked.

"What?" Mary retorted, "Do all fat, white girls look the same to you?"

"W-well, no," you stammered, "but you sort of look like you could be from the same tribe."

"We *are* sisters," Vicky said. "She's just pulling your leg."

The three of you studied together for the entire quarter. All three of you got A's. The only A's in the class that finally ended up having fifteen students. You took Mary and Vicky as signs, signs that you should major in philosophy rather than English. The three of you took several classes together over the next year, and the three of you always headed the class.

After graduation, you got a job working for a bank as a programmer trainee. That was the beginning. Back then, there were no degrees in Computer Science. Now, some years and many, many projects later, you are some richer, some heavier, more tired, and still at a loss to explain how it all happened.

Compound that with having almost just lost it all because of some asshole trying to pen a crime on you, and life seems like one big crap shoot. And maybe the man was right. It all seems to signify nothing.

In the car heading back home, you ask Phyllis, "What the fuck is the point of it all?"

"There is no point."

"I mean . . .."

"I know what you mean," he cuts you off. "You mean what is the point of life."

"Exactly!"

"The answer is the same."

"Then why do we keep trying?"

"Why do lemmings run to the sea? It's what they do."

"You mean we do it 'cause we do it?" you ask.

"Right," he answers. "No good, no bad, just life."

You can see the sun sliding behind a bank of clouds in the western sky. You cruise along the expressway looking at the neighborhoods you pass through. Slums give way to middle class houses, and they eventually turn to mansions and estates.

"That sucks," you say, "that . . . really . . . sucks."

About the author

Larry Redmond is a native of Chicago, Illinois. He graduated from Hyde Park High School and served in the U.S. Air Force. He did his basic training at Lackland Air Force Base (AFB) in San Antonio, Texas, then went for further training at Goodfellow AFB in San Angelo, Texas. He was stationed in Darmstadt, Germany, for three years working in intelligence.

After a short return to the U.S. where he worked at several odd jobs including six months as an assembler for an electronics company near Mt. Vernon, New York, he spend 15 months traveling in Europe where he hitch-hiked from Lapland in Scandinavia to Morocco in North Africa working along the way at a variety of jobs from farm hand to factory worker to dishwasher to carpenter's assistant, mainly in Sweden and Germany. His travels have taken him to Oslo, Norway; Copenhagen, Denmark; Amsterdam, the Netherlands; Paris, France; Cologne, Germany; Barcelona, Spain; and Tangier, Morocco.

Upon his return to the United States he attended the University of Illinois at Chicago, where he majored in Philosophy and minored in English. He did further graduate work and later attended the John Marshall Law School, earning a Juris Doctor degree. He has also done graduate work in Computer Science and Telecommunications at De Paul University. He has worked in Chicago and throughout the United States as a computer consultant designing and implementing fault-tolerant application in a wide range in industries from banking to transportation to manufacturing. He has worked as a criminal defense attorney representing high-profile death row inmates, several of whom were released pursuant to DNA testing. He has been active in third-party politics.

He has also found time for a full and rich family life, with seven children and one grandchild. His hobbies include physical training and martial arts, African and Conga drumming, and yoga and meditation.

He currently works and lives with his family in Chicago.

Visit on-line at www.LarryRedmond.com for other books by Larry Redmond